THE
CANDLEMAKER'S
MERMAN

Grey Liliy

ISBN-13: 978-1943161027
ISBN-10: 194316102X

Cover by Grey Liliy

CHAPTER 1

THE CREATURE WOULD not stop staring at him.

Phillip worked on the knots as best he could, his fingers slipping from sweat against the rough texture of the rope. With death-like, black eyes staring at him from the water below, his nerves felt like they were on fire. You'd think someone who ate and prepared fish every day of his life would be used to empty fish eyes staring at him. Then again, these were the eyes of a shark. Completely different, if you asked Phillip. Fish eyes at least had something other than a gaping black void in their eye sockets.

Phillip squeezed his thighs together as he straddled the giant wooden water gate. It was held shut by thick ropes strung together in a jumbled mess of knots tied by someone who didn't know what they were doing and just wanted it to stay tied. Would it have killed the fishery to at least have one of the sailors tie this thing closed? Phillip grunted as he leaned over and tugged one of the loops loose.

His shark tooth necklace fell out of his shirt, and Phillip stuffed it back under the fabric as quickly as it had come out. Knowing his luck, the string would break and it'd fall into the water below with that monster.

Phillip could just cut the darned rope off with his knife, but that would give him away and provide evidence of tampering. He was already grateful any knot he tied back would be just as good as what he found. It just wasn't possible to remember exactly what this monstrosity of rope looked like before he untied it.

Speaking of monsters:

Phillip glanced down into the pool next to him, just past the edge of his buckled shoes. The creature swam beneath him, circling and still staring. The fishery had caught the creature by accident with a fishing net, all seven feet of pure muscle and mythology. Knowing they had to keep this prize at all cost, they threw the beast squirming from the net into the closed off fish farm; the only thing they had big enough to hold the beast.

In that short time from fishing net to tank, the monster had killed three people. The first got his throat ripped out by the creature's sharp teeth when it lunged from the netting. The second was slashed through the side —bled to death later—with clawed fingers as he squirmed and lashed out. And the third suffocated when the creature dragged him down into the tank when they dumped him from the net. Phillip hadn't seen it up close until now, but he knew what the water hid below was dangerous.

The merman.

Phillip didn't think he resembled the merman in stories he had heard when he was a child. They were supposed to be beautiful and enchanting, more fish like, and less like a wild eating machine. Though, all Phillip could see from his seat on the top edge of the wooden wall was the creature's head and the tips of the dorsal fin on its back. It had the upper torso of a man, skin a lighter grey in color than the rest, and the lower half of a shark. Phillip couldn't see much more than that, which ultimately didn't matter. Because its eyes were definitely that of a shark shoved into a human's head and they *would not stop staring at him!*

Phillip threw the rope down and ran his fingers through his hair. He leant over the edge of the wooden wall, and looked into the deep pit filled with black water. "Look, I know you don't like me or us and what not, but I'm doing my very best to get you out by undoing the knot on this door, and you're making it very difficult for me to concentrate! Please, please just go under the water or look the other way or something so I can get the gate open and we never have to see each other again."

Phillip breathed heavily after finishing his speech, his fingers gripping the edge of the wooden door hard enough that his hands hurt. The creature dipped under the water and disappeared from view, much to his relief. Phillip went back to the knot, looking over his shoulder to make sure his spontaneous plea hadn't drawn attention from anyone else with legs.

Blocked off by thick wooden beams and alongside the open bay, the area was far from the main fishery and living quarters. Not many came down here unless they were going to see the merman, and most of them had sense to wait until daylight when you could actually see him.

4

The darkness hid the creature quite well, and candles could only do so much from such a height. The same height that kept the creature down below trapped in this oversized fish tank. There was a good ten feet from the top of the water to the top of the wooden gate, and it was secured with the most piss poor ropes Phillip had ever seen, and he made candles all day!

Phillip glanced at the still surface of the water, tugging on the edge of a loose loop of rope. It rippled quietly, ominously, still hiding the dangerous predator underneath. Phillip would not deny he was losing his mind by doing this, but it had to be done.

In total, the merman in the tank had taken the lives of eight people. The five murders outside of the net transfer, were poor souls whose deaths doubled as the creature's meals. The fish that previously occupied the farm tank were long gone, lost to its voracious appetite. Sharks couldn't tell much of a difference between white and red meat it seemed. Not that the deaths of those men were reported as his feeding time. They were reported as "accidents." People who got too close to the edge and fell. As if that would happen five times, but no one dared question the sheriff.

The sheriff took well to the offered bribe money from the owner of the fishery, Boris, and that was that. They were using that monster as a spectacle and a fear tactic and it twisted Phillip's gut the wrong way. He was used to the fishery owner making people disappear; it was why he was still in charge. But Phillip couldn't stop that.

This, this was different. That creature down there was something else entirely, and it gave Phillip the absolute creeps. They were messing with something they didn't understand, and he was going to make sure it was gone before it could take the lives of more innocents.

Or invade his nightmares again.

Phillip had been delivering candles when the fourth person to be sacrificed to it had been thrown in the tank. The boss of the fishery hadn't seen him, but Phillip could see plenty. The blood and the flesh torn from bones had been the most brutal thing he had ever seen. Even from a distance, there was no mistaking the ripped limbs and the sheer amount of *red* that had darkened the water. Phillip had run home that night, delivery forgotten.

Nightmares plagued the candlemaker every day after. His wife was on the verge of kicking him out onto the dirt floor of their sitting area if he tossed and turned one more time. He calmed himself, justifying that it was no different from any other death-by-boss that occurred on their island. It was after the fifth death had been reported that the nightmares came back full force. Phillip made up his mind right then to break open the gate and get rid of the fishery boss' prized pet, life on the line or not!

Sleep was something he just couldn't afford to give up.

Phillip grinned when he finally managed to get the first knot undone. He looked down to the water when he felt a slight chill on his back. The creature was peeking up at him slightly from the corner, only the top of his high cheekbones and up visible. His glaring wasn't quite as intense as before, replaced with an almost thoughtful gaze. Phillip rubbed his mouth with the back of his hand and went back to work. "Just two more knots and you're out of here."

Phillip was almost through the last knot when he heard the loud footsteps echoing on the creaking wooden planks that made up the high pier around the edges of the enclosure. Caught, Phillip got to his feet just in time for a meaty hand to wrap itself around his throat, lifting Phillip clear off his feet. His captor dragged him back over to the wider pier from the tank gate, his footsteps' heavy thumps rattling the thin walkway. Phillip struggled, but to his dismay, he was only a slim man of five feet and six inches, while the man holding him clearly surpassed six feet with the fat and weight behind him to near double it.

They always did call Mark "The Giant" behind his back for a reason.

Phillip smacked the brute's arm, using his very best parent voice. He prayed it would be enough authority to hold true with the dumber man. "Let go!"

"What on earth do you think you're doin'?" Mark asked, looking down at the merman as he held the tiny candlemaker in place. The creature hissed up at him, teeth bared. Mark looked at the undone knots on the gate that lead out to the open water, and chuckled, proud he put two and two together. He always thought it was funny the only thing separating the scary thing down below from where he wanted to go was a thick piece of wood and a gate, but that was an amusement for another day. Right now, Mark's attention was taken by Phillip. "Trying to let the boss' pet go? Now why would ya' do a thing like that?"

"He shouldn't be here!" Phillip pointed down. Mark wasn't the brightest thinker, so it was possible he could be reasoned with. *Treat him like your son and you can do this, Phillip!* "The boss has had five men killed because of it! That's five more than he usually kills in a month! Just about anything sets him off lately. Who's next do you think? When will it be you or me?"

"I don't know about me," Mark replied, scratching his chin with rough nails. He did like the candlemaker because he always gave Mark an extra small one for his kid's nightlight. But the boss would be even more happy if Mark saved his pet. Making the boss happy always took priority. Mark patted the candlemaker on the shoulder, "But I think yours is today."

"Wait!" Phillip yelled as Mark held him over the edge of the water, the merman swimming in a wide circle below, watching the exchange. Memories of blood filling the water in streams and torn limbs floating to the top filled the artisan's head. Phillip grasped at Mark's hand and pleaded with the loyal moron. "What are you doing? Don't drop me!"

"Seems to me," Mark said, holding the candlemaker out over the water. The small man squirmed, uselessly hitting his hands. Mark felt a little bad, but the hope of praise from Boris was going to be worth it. Mark though himself rather witty when he added, "If you like the guy down there so much to risk your life letting him go, ya' should pay him a visit."

Phillip dropped like a rock when Mark released him, hitting the water like a cracked egg to a skillet. The cold liquid rushed into his lungs, plastering his short blonde hair to his head and weighing his clothes down.

Phillip managed to pull himself to the surface, gasping in a breath of air, limbs flailing in a panic. He swam to the side to try and grab onto a rivet or anything to keep himself upright, latching to the wooden side walls like a wet cat. Mark laughed at him from above and after a few moments, Phillip felt the shaking of the tank side as he walked away.

Mark wasn't going to watch. Phillip nearly cried out for help, a last plea of mercy, but he stopped with his mouth wide open when he felt *its* presence behind him.

CHAPTER 2

PHILLIP TURNED SLOWLY in the water, finding himself face to face with the creature responsible for his night terrors. Barely an inch between them, Phillip got a good view of the merman's face. Eyes black as coal with not a lick of white to be seen, stared him down and held him in place. He broke hold from the gaze to focus on something else. Phillip recognized the grey skin from the distance, but now that he was close he could tell the creature's hair color. It was a dark shade of red that hung down near the bottom of his neck, flattened by the weight of the water it carried.

The creature had a scar running diagonally across its face, gills at its neck, and he could see a row of teeth much like his own, only all of them were triangular, sharp and serrated. It had a mouth full of teeth that matched the shark's tooth that hung around his own neck. The candlemaker would have grabbed at the necklace, but he needed both hands to defend himself should it move too quickly. Futile as though such an effort may be. Phillip could now see the entire upper body was made of lean muscle that bled into a shark's tail. Everything about this monster was equally powerful. Phillip realized the distance between them was lessening and took a breath. This was not how he expected to di—

"I know I'm gorgeous, but do you really have to keep staring?" The merman quipped, enjoying the yelp the man made at the sound of his voice. The human's eyes widened as large as clamshells and he was quite close to hyperventilating. As he should be! This merman was a fearsome lord of the deep! Humans *should* cower at his very being. The merman raised both arms out of the water in a proper shrug, impersonating the man's tone of voice from earlier. "It's making it *very* difficult to

8

concentrate."

"You have one hand," Phillip blurted, noting that the merman's right arm ended at the wrist. He wore a sort of brass covering over the stump where a hand had been, presumably, cut off at some point.

The merman glanced down at his stump and back up at the human slowly, as if the man before him was a complete and total idiot. The merman blinked once, retracting the nictitating membrane from his eyes. The eyes underneath the black coating were human-like with an oval pupil.

The merman laughed, dropping his arms back into the water with a splash and a flick of his tail. "What? No 'You can talk!' first?"

"Uh, right," Phillip said. He sunk into the water about an inch, feeling oddly embarrassed for some reason. Seeing as he wasn't being torn limb from limb, and that the creature before him was far less frightening when his eyes were a russet color, Phillip decided to be polite. "Sorry, my son has one hand and you're the first person I've seen who matches."

"Oh?" The merman grinned waving his arm back and forth. Missing limbs were pretty normal for his folks, so he figured it was similar for humans, but apparently that was not the case. Most of the time humans and merman had more in common than he'd care to admit on the best of days, so it was nice to see the divide again. Mermen being the superior group and all. Granted, usually they're also a little older when they lose a limb. The man before him was far too young to have offspring *that* old just yet. The man only looked five or so years older than himself! "What happened to him? I doubt his got bitten off in a fight, or are humans more adventurous than I've noticed?"

"He got hurt, and w-we." Phillip pulled hair out of his face, stomach turning as he remembered the doctor sawing at his little boy's hand. He licked his lips, thinking of his son's muffled screaming. "We couldn't save it—wait a second! You can talk. Why didn't you talk before?"

"Wasn't to my advantage," the merman said. He tried to hide his amusement at the sudden change in subject. The merman dropped his gaze to the side, staring at a metal bolt screwed into the wood. "Sometimes it's better if they think you're a dumb beast."

Phillip nodded, shivering from the cold water. He rubbed at his upper arm to put the feeling back into it, while still trying to hold onto the wall. "I see."

"And right now, it's to my advantage that I can tell you what to do."

The merman grinned and slapped Phillip on the back with his palm, careful to keep his fingers up. Wouldn't want to scratch him before the human made himself useful. "You see, your buddy left because he thinks that I'm going to eat you."

"Are you?"

The merman smacked him upside the head, this time not caring if his claws hit him. "I will if you keep asking stupid questions! Now pay attention!"

"Right," Phillip rubbed the spot where he had been whacked, wondering if he maybe was in fact already dead. Perhaps he was being eaten alive this very moment, and this whole thing about talking with the monstrous merman like he was a new client visiting the shop was a delusion to spare him the agony. Or it could be real. Phillip supposed either way it beat the agony of being beaten alive. *Carrying on then!* "Sorry."

"As I was saying, the only reason *I* can't get out of this ridiculous fish tank of theirs would be the no legs and one hand thing." He tapped the human's cheek with his stump to emphasize his point. "I can't pull myself up and out."

Phillip nodded, though he was aware of this fact already.

"You, however, are not only the first person interested in helping me out, but also have two legs and two hands and could probably climb out if I gave you a boost up." The merman pointed to the top of the gate. "You think you can finish undoing those knots if I get you up?"

Phillip studied the gated walls of the fish farm. Between the small open spaces between the boards and the metal sheets bolted into them to keep its shape, there were plenty of hand holds to climb out. "Yeah, I should be able to. It doesn't look like Mark retied them when he left."

"Great!" The merman grabbed him by the waist and ducked them both down under the water, the human struggling. He used his tail to thrust them both up in a jump that gave them an extra three feet of reach. Phillip managed to grab onto a loose plank in his wild flailing, the merman delightfully amused by his panic, and used his feet on the jutting rivets to get a proper foothold. He had another two or three feet before he could grab a proper ledge to pull himself up, but it was better than being down below. The merman called up after him, "You think you can get yourself up?"

"Yeah!" Phillip struggled to the top, one board and rivet at a time.

After an agonizing five minutes, he collapsed on the top of the frame with a wet plop, water dripping down the sides from his soaked clothes. Phillip checked behind him on the flat pier to make sure Mark hadn't returned yet, and got back to work on the knots. "I'm in so much trouble after this."

"I gathered," the merman agreed. He was honestly a little surprised the human was still cooperating. Shaking, cold to the touch, about to be dead whether or not the merman ate him, and he was still up there trying to get the gate open. For all intents and purposes, the human was digging himself further into the grave with no sign of reward for himself. The merman sunk an inch into the water. "Why are you helping, anyway? You're clearly terrified."

"That's why," Phillip said, back to working on the knots. His hands shivered, desperately trying to return some warmth with the frenzied movement. He wanted warm clothes and to be in his bed. "You scare me. Terrify me actually, despite our lovely conversation at this moment. But how I feel about it doesn't change the fact that you shouldn't be here."

"That's true," The merman said wading next to the gate. The human had blond hair, green eyes and a fair complexion that could probably use more sun. Plain shirt, brown pants, and shoes with metal buckles. There was also an odd apron of some sort the merman didn't recognize from the other humans that milled around his watery prison. "So what do you do in this wonderful complex of horrors?"

"I make candles." Phillip pulled out a particularly tough loop, and grinned being one step closer to victory. "The fishery goes through enough with night work that they need a full time candlemaker in-house."

"Candles? Remind me which human trinket that is again?" The merman scrunched his face, searching his memories. "I'm pretty familiar with your boating equipment, but that term seems to escape me."

"It's a light source. You've probably seen one inside of a lantern. They hold a tiny flame for a few hours using wax and a wick." Phillip grunted at another particularly annoying knot. "They're handy, but it takes forever to make them properly with the wax."

"So it's a skilled job?" The merman wondered how someone could be smart enough for skilled labor but still seem so simple. He seemed too nice to be in a place like this. "That takes brains?"

"Yes, not that it'll save me once Mark tells the boss what I've done."

Phillip made plans in his head. After this he'd have to grab his wife and his son and all the money they could and just run until they left town. Hopefully Sarah would at least wait until after they escaped the island to take her turn in line murdering him.

"Maybe not," the merman said. "If he lives near the water I can promise you won't have to worry about him."

The human flinched at the suggestion. The merman snorted bubbles in the water. *Definitely too nice.*

The blond worked on the knots for two more minutes, and the merman was already bored out of his skull. He swished his tail around in the water, watching his pelvic fin of all things, as he did his best to appear less threatening. The skittish human was his only ticket out of here, so having him change his mind at the last second was not an option. "But enough about me, you mentioned having a little one at home?"

"Yes," Phillip answered absently. He sniffed, rubbing the back of his hand against his nose before going back to tugging on the ropes. "My little Icarus, which is not the name I chose by the way. He's turned three this year, and it's a miracle in itself that he still lives and breathes."

The merman looked at his brass covering plate, and thinking of an infant with a matching wound. "Sickly thing?"

"More or less," Phillip said. He pictured his little boy's bright smile, and felt one form on his own face, even through the shivers and the gaze of an underwater beast. Phillip tugged harder on a rope. "But he's *my* sickly boy and I plan to keep him alive as long as possible, and I know his mother agrees with me."

The merman nodded in appreciation. "Pretty wife?"

"No."

The merman jolted in place and snorted out a laugh. The answer had been so blunt and straight forward he couldn't help himself. "Wow, that's a first. What sort of husband doesn't say his wife is pretty?"

"One who likes to tell the truth," Phillip laughed, moving on to the third knot that held the gate closed. "She's not ugly though, more average than anything. It was an arranged marriage, so save for our little boy, we have nothing in common. I don't even think she likes me, truth be told."

"Bet that makes the bedroom fun."

"Hey!" Phillip shouted, grabbing the ropes as he almost fell from the shock of the question. The creature laughed at him, and Phillip would rather his personal life be off the table for the moment. "I think that's enough about me. What do, did, you do in your free time?"

The merman shrugged. "What does any other shark do? I swim and eat."

"Nothing else?" Phillip tilted his head. "What about other mermen? Don't you all have hobbies or a society or something?"

"We're not talking about them."

Phillip took the stern tone of voice as a hint, and went back to untying the last knot. He worked silently as they both sat, tense and hoping no one else would interrupt. It took Phillip another five minutes, but he managed to break the last knot and kick the gate open. It moved slowly, trying to push the water out of the way, but soon there was a good three foot gap for the creature to slip through. The merman was out of the gate before Phillip could so much as sit on the edge. "Well, that's one part done."

The merman relished the taste of the open water. It was the same water that had filtered into his holding area, but not nearly as stale. The currents pulled and rushed through his gills in a way he had dearly missed, and he would never take this rush of water for granted again. The merman looked up at the human, sitting on the edge of the wooden gate watching, and smirked.

Phillip hadn't been prepared for the merman to turn around and swim straight for the pen. The merman rammed into the side, rattling the entire wall hard enough that Phillip fell off the edge and into the water. He had a slight feeling of *déjà vu* as he swam himself through to the thick surface.

Phillip turned in time to see the merman pin his chest to the gate wall with the forearm of his handless limb, and watched in horror as the other clawed hand jammed itself into the top of his chest, just below his shoulder. Phillip cried out as claws dug their way down, leaving five long deep impressions in his flesh stopping just above his naval. The blood flowed freely into the water and the merman released him after a moment of admiring his work.

Phillip held at the wall at a crossbeam with one hand, and his chest best he could with the other, trying to shove his shirt into the wound to stop the bleeding. The open wound stung unmercifully thanks to the salted water around him in addition to the torn flesh. Phillip felt justified by shouting, "What was that for!"

The merman cut the man off by covering the human's mouth with his hand.

"Just a reminder that you're off limits should we meet again," the merman grinned, the poor man now *very* terrified. "I may forget what color hair you have or your eyes or your name, but I never forget my handiwork."

Phillip exhaled deeply when the creature dipped below the water with a flash and out of sight. His chest stung, he was cold and wet, but he was alive. Phillip rubbed the raw skin around the bleeding gashes as the merman disappeared in the distance. He dropped his head against the wooden gate behind him to collect himself.

Phillip swam toward the dock a moment later, ignoring the pain and smell of blood. *Could have been worse.*

CHAPTER 3

A DAY LATER, Phillip lifted his heavy delivery pole up and over his shoulder. The candles that hung along its length by their un-cut wicks swung back and forth lightly hitting into each other with soft waxy thuds. When it came to cherishing the little things in life, Phillip considered walking along the river that bisected the town with his product as definitely one of them.

Phillip's island was home to around three thousand people, most crammed like sardines into small one or two room houses that made up their town. The island was split lengthways down the middle by a river, with two major dirt roads on either side of the rushing water. There was only one bridge that connected the two sides, however, so foot traffic across was heavy with homes on one side and the main fishery and shops on the other. The island itself was small enough that someone could walk from one end to the other in about an hour, give or take, at a regular pace.

The surrounding waters were full of tall rocks and outcroppings that made ships entering and leaving dangerous enough that the island was forced to be as self sufficient as possible. That independence from the mainland was the biggest reason as to why Boris held so much power in the community for so long. His fishery was responsible for not only feeding, but also employing, everyone on the island who didn't specialize in a trade.

And even then, while there were at least two or three people per each major trade, at least one worked for the fishery to keep their own in-house standards as self-sufficient as the island's small economy. Outside trade was a once a year event when the mainland boat made its annual appearance.

As such, Phillip had gotten quite skilled at haggling for leftovers from the butcher to get a supply of tallow for his candles. Phillip longed for a decent supply of spermaceti, but knew better than to push his luck getting it on the current supply list. Thankfully, he knew that the only other candlemaker on the other side of the island had the same issue.

And neither of them were any better off than the butcher who longed for three or more cows so he could sell more meat once a week without waiting for little baby calves to grow up. Phillip chuckled to himself thinking of the poor folks drooling over cattle that still needed to procreate before they could eat them. It was nice to know he was in good company in longing for supplies.

Phillip had the luck of being the in-house candlemaker for the fishery, but today he was delivering candles made during his off hours to a local shop to sell. Every little bit of income helped when you were raising a son that was chronically ill and needed fresh bandages daily when his wound decided to fester. Phillip had mastered the ability to make his candles burn about two hours longer than the one other candlemaker on the island, so he always managed to pick up one or two of the more savvy customers from his competitor.

Phillip still had this privilege because he was still alive.

How had he survived letting the boss' prized possession of the moment and main tool of intimidation escape? Why, that was easy: Mark was rather terrified of Phillip at the moment.

So much so, that Mark vowed not to tell the boss that Phillip had been the one to open the gate. There had even been a bit of pleading on his knees to be spared. After he had dragged himself out of the water, Phillip had been walking back through the warehouse when he ran into Mark, who had been on his way to double check that Phillip was indeed fish-food. However, upon seeing Phillip whole and well, Mark dropped to his aforementioned knees and almost started to sob.

Phillip had been a bit confused over this at first (and embarrassed that standing full height Phillip was still only tall enough to be eye level with Mark on his knees), but after looking down at his bleeding chest, he realized something important: Mark thought he beat up the killer shark-monster. Phillip had walked away from a monster that had ripped apart eight other men twice his size. As such, Mark was quick to make his own assumptions and Phillip decided he was welcome to them. Mark firmly decided to get out of his way and keep his mouth shut.

Phillip wondered how long that would last, but either way, none of that mattered because his wife was still livid over the entire ordeal.

Not that he completely blamed her.

Her husband was injured to the point he had to take a day off work, and in a single night threatened to destroy himself, his family and everything he'd worked for over what amounted to her as "a fish." Sarah was currently not talking to him, but Phillip was happy she at least helped bandage his chest before going off to the other side of the house and not talk to him.

Boris was furious about the whole thing, too, but thanks to Mark keeping his mouth shut, Phillip was in the clear and out of the boss' line of sight. No one even so much as suspected that he'd even gone near the creature, let alone that he'd been brave enough to open the gates. Which meant for now, he had nothing to worry about.

Except the merman grinning at him from the boat dock.

Phillip nearly dropped his supply of candles as he passed one of the many short river docks cutting into the water. The merman had pulled himself up on the low wood, resting his head on crossed arms, tail hanging below. The creature's dorsal and pectoral fins were visible as he hung from the side of the dock. The daylight revealed a large gash along the merman's back Phillip hadn't noticed before, as well as a plethora of other scratches and scrapes in the merman's rough skin. Phillip subconsciously rubbed at his bandaged chest and looked back down at the merman.

"Hello," Phillip trailed off, not sure if calling the creature "merman" was rude or not. So he went for something safe: "I don't think I caught your name."

"To be fair, I didn't ask for yours either," the merman said. The human had a long pole draped over his shoulder, the length of it covered in hanging candles. The merman was proud to recognize them after he had looked them up! The poor man's feet were twitching slightly, like he was a single breath away from sprinting. He reminded the merman of a minnow sitting still one moment before flitting away with a flash of light against its scales. The merman asked, "Long time no see?"

"It's been less than two days," Phillip answered bluntly, double checking that there was a good ten feet between him and the merman. He hadn't been harmed too much from their last encounter, but Phillip had not forgotten how easily his chest had been torn open the last time they met. "I thought you marked me so you wouldn't forget me years later."

"What can I say? I was bored." The merman shrugged. It was true. He *had* been bored. Plus, he still needed to find out where the man who had imprisoned him lived. The fact the man's blood hadn't been split yet for the embarrassment the merman had suffered was downright criminal. "So, name?"

"Phillip." He waited a beat. "And yours would be?"

"Pistol." The merman flipped his tail to the side kicking up a splash of water. The droplets almost reached the man standing on the shore.

"Pistol?" Phillip wrapped the word around his tongue like particularly rotten piece of meat. "Really? Your named after a pistol? As in a gun?"

"It's a good name!" Pistol huffed, glaring at the other man. "At least it's not something dorky like 'Phillip.' "

"My name isn't—No, never mind." Phillip rubbed the side of his temple and shook his head. The merman tapped his claws on the edge of the dock, making little clicks on the wood. Phillip looked around, remembering he was on a main street and the merman was in plain sight. "What are you doing out here, anyway? Are you trying to get caught again?"

"The first time was a fluke!" Pistol shouted. He had gotten caught before because he had chosen the wrong place to take a nap. He wouldn't be living down that incident any time soon, and he'd be damned if the nice guy up there reminded him of it *again*. Pistol's friends rubbed it in his face more than enough. Besides, soon he'd have the problem taken care of himself. Pistol pulled his fingers into a fist, scraping five long gashes into the wood of the dock. "It won't be happening again, I can assure you."

Phillip took an extra step back from the water, feet firmly planted on the dirt road that ran alongside the water's edge. Sensing the vicious man eater in a bad mood, Phillip changed the subject. "So, you swim in rivers often?"

"No," *Idiot,* "not often. I only venture down river when I need to talk to skittish candlemakers who should really come closer so I can stop shouting!"

"I'd prefer to stay where I am, thank you," Phillip said, hitching his pole higher on his shoulder. The candles that hung on the edges swayed in the breeze, free to move about on the empty street. *It was awfully dead out on the main road today, wasn't it?* Phillip asked himself. "Don't take this the wrong way, but I rather like living and you seem to be in a bad temper today."

Fair enough, Pistol thought. He shifted to hold himself up with his elbow, and waved a hand at the edge of the dirt road. The road edge was about a foot from the edge of the river, and was raised about three feet above the water. "Could you at least get to the edge of the drop off then? It's not like I can grab you from there."

Phillip eyed the distance between the top of the road and the river water a few feet down. It seemed like there was enough distance to keep safe, but he'd also seen Pistol jump higher than that in the fish tank. Phillip edged closer as a small sign of good faith, but still kept a good foot from the edge. "Well, what is it you needed?"

"The address of your boss. And if he doesn't live near open water, which docks does he spend the most time at?" Pistol smiled, showing off his pearly whites, at the verge of outright licking his teeth or flat out drooling. "I owe him a word or two."

Phillip shook his head slowly, the merman's intentions very clear. "No. I'm sorry, and I know that he's a horrible person and all, but that doesn't give me the right to help aid someone else kill him."

Pistol frowned, "He was going to kill you! He imprisoned me! The guy's got it coming."

"I'm sorry, but I can't help you do that. Just, just let it be and go back home."

"I can't!"

"Well neither can I!" During his exchange, Phillip never noticed that he had gotten closer and closer to the edge of the dirt, in his efforts to talk some sense into the merman. Nothing good would come of killing the fishery owner in cold blood, no matter how much he deserved it. In fact, Phillip was fairly certain it would make things a thousand times worse, and he had no time to explain that to a temperamental merman. So Phillip went with the basics: "Murder is wrong!"

"This isn't murder! It's revenge!" Pistol argued back. He dropped off the dock and swam up until he was right in front of the candlemaker. He made sure to look Phillip in the eye, despising that he had to look up to do so. Pistol smacked both of his limbs into the water creating a splash worthy of a tantrum throwing child. "I can't let this go!"

Phillip nearly whined at the merman, almost in disbelief their argument had been reduced to this bickering. "Why not?"

"I'll never live it down if I don't kill him!" Pistol ducked down under the surface of the water. A few moments later he pushed up, easily jumping the three feet needed to grab Phillip by the ankle.

Pistol pulled.

The merman dragged Phillip into the water, dropping his pole and candles on the side of the road. Once again, he was submerged completely under the water and had to struggle to the surface for breath. For two seconds he thought he was going to die again by the hands of the merman when Phillip took notice that Pistol was only glaring at him and not ripping him to shreds.

Phillip was reminded of a particularly bratty teenager, and for the first time noticed how young Pistol looked. If he were human, he'd probably be about nineteen or twenty at the oldest. Phillip pushed his hair out of his eyes. "What was that for?"

"I was tired of yelling up," Pistol jabbed a finger into Phillip's chest. "Now tell me where your boss hangs out that's near the water."

Phillip scrunched his face in anger and resisted the urge to throw water in Pistol's face. "No."

"Do I have to threaten you?" Pistol asked, showing off his claws and teeth, "because I can do things that way, too."

"Yes," Phillip sucked in a breath and steeled himself. "Monster or not, I won't be a part of a murder!"

Pistol snorted. He really should just kill the guy and be done with it, but he didn't want to. Phillip glared at him, green eyes bright and determined. Pistol huffed. Would be pretty pointless to even threaten to eat the loser; Pistol wouldn't do it. There was something about Phillip that made Pistol lose his appetite. "Jerk."

"I think that's you," Phillip said, looking up at the shore. He grabbed a clod of dirt and started to pull himself up. "At least my candles didn't get wet."

Phillip was halfway out of the water, when he felt Pistol grab the front of his shirt and yank him back down with another splash. "Hey!"

Pistol ignored him and reached under the shirt for the necklace he had seen from the side as Phillip climbed out of the water. He pulled the string around the man's neck, tugging out the shark's tooth. A decent sized one, it was just a bit larger than Pistol's thumb. The merman looked up at the candlemaker and grinned. "What's a guy like you doing with a shark's tooth?"

Phillip felt the blush color his cheeks, and grabbed his necklace back. Phillip hadn't taken it off, save to replace the string once or twice, since he first made the necklace. "I found it on the beach when I was kid."

"Huh." Pistol snickered, trying to imagine Mr. Murder-is-Wrong carrying around a symbol of one of the ocean's most deadly predators. "And you were aware of what it was when you started to wear it, right?"

"Yes!" Phillip snorted, embarrassment growing. "My dad told me and I thought it was neat."

Since then, his necklace had sort of developed into a bit of a security blanket. Whenever he was worried or nervous, he only had to think of it around his neck to be secure. Phillip fingered the necklace, turning it over in his fingers. He hadn't thought of it once after being dragged in the water by Pistol. Phillip glanced at the merman, watching him with a humored look about him.

Maybe the living thing the tooth was attached to worked just as well.

"Is there something wrong with liking sharks' teeth?" Phillip asked shoving the necklace back under his shirt. "I mean, you've got a whole mouthful of them."

"So you like my mouth?"

"That is not what I said!"

Pistol laughed. Again. He'd give Phillip one thing, simple minded or not, he did make Pistol laugh. That was more than enough reason for the merman to want him to stay alive. Pistol shoved him in the shoulder, amused by the man's pout. "You're too easy."

"So I've been told," Phillip said, moving his hair out of his face again. "Now if you don't mind, I need to—"

"Daddy!" A young boy shouted, leaning over the edge of the road. He stood proudly wearing his pants and shirt that matched his daddy's. His waist coast was tied too tightly in the back, though, his skin itching just under the fabric. Mommy was always doing that. The boy got closer to the side, hoping to get a better view of his daddy in the water. "Daddy!"

"Icarus! Get away from that edge!" Phillip shouted up, concerned for his tiny son's balance. He felt the water splash against him, and Phillip glanced out the corner of his eye to see Pistol had dipped under the surface and swam close to the edge out of sight. "You'll fall, son!"

"Daddy!" Icarus repeated, proud of his word. So proud, he decided to show off a second. "Wet!"

"Yes, daddy's all wet," Phillip laughed and started to climb up the bank, this time far more successful. It seemed Pistol had no intention of showing himself to Phillip's son, and for that he was oddly grateful. "What are you doing out here?"

"We were going to the market," Sarah answered, walking up behind the boy. She grabbed Icarus' hand and pulled him back from the edge. Her little boy nibbled the bandages wrapped around his stub on the other wrist. She sighed, squatting down to pull the limb out of the boy's mouth. It was worse than sucking his thumb, and a habit even harder to break. Sarah glared down at her hopeless husband. "What on earth were you doing in the water, Phillip?"

"Ah, I thought I saw something moving and slipped when I got a closer look," Phillip said, biting his lip. "Sorry, Sarah."

"You need to watch where you're going," she sighed. There was no helping that man at all. She only hoped her son inherited traits from her side of the family as he grew older. Phillip's family history was a lost cause. "Pick up your candles and get moving or you'll be late."

"Yes, dear," Phillip said, reaching down to pluck his son from the ground in a quick hug. He dropped the boy to his feet and allowed him to go back to his mother's skirt. "Have a nice shopping trip."

Sarah shook her head and continued on their walk. She noticed her husband staring at the river water as he continued and sighed to herself. He'd probably fall in again before the day was out. After his last dip in the water with that monster, one would think the man would stay clear of it. Sarah gripped Icarus' hand tightly and picked up her pace. That wouldn't happen. She knew there was little that would keep Phillip away from the water completely.

Phillip was more fascinated by the water than he realized, even to himself.

Sarah and Icarus disappeared ahead, at a much faster pace toward the market. Phillip stayed close behind, and breathed easy after a few more minutes. There was no sign of Pistol after his wife and son rounded the bend around the nearest building. Phillip collected his candles, thankful only two had snapped in half, and started down the street again. Phillip had a feeling that wasn't the last he'd be seeing of Pistol.

The dorsal fin that ran across the river water unseen behind Phillip was proof of that.

CHAPTER 4

"YOU'RE GOING TO be the death of me, I can feel it," Phillip hissed down at the merman swimming along the river parallel to the road.

Pistol's eyes glowed in the moonlight, like a cat in the dark, as he swam along with his head above the water. Phillip's client had conned him into helping set up his store display, so Phillip was stuck walking home long after sunset. He would have lit a candle, but Phillip couldn't afford to waste the product. Pistol grinned up at him from the water, free to pester him, and Phillip cursed the small population of his island and their tendency to be inside once the moon was out.

"If you would just tell me where I could find your boss, I'd leave you alone," Pistol said, watching as the human tried to ignore him. Phillip walked stiffly, forcing his head to stay forward. That was fine, Pistol could dig a challenge. Until he got his revenge, he had nothing but time on his hands, anyway. Pistol rubbed a spot on his arm where his leader Slate had scratched him, the new raw wound a reminder that his clan still wasn't happy with him. Until he killed Phillip's boss, Pistol was doomed to remain at the bottom of the pecking order. He didn't know how to function in last place. "I can do this all day, every day."

"I'm not helping," Phillip said, shifting his pole to a more comfortable position. Pistol swam ahead until he was alongside, head and shoulders now fully above the water. His dorsal fin and the tip of his tail fin hung ominously out of the water just behind, reminding Phillip of Pistol's shark half. "I am sorry, but there's nothing I can do about it. So go home."

"Why not?" Pistol asked, before huffing. There had to be something he could give or do for Phillip to get a little cooperation. Compensation for

Phillip's information to override the fear of getting caught had to exist! Pistol swam a little faster to get ahead of the man, he turned to swim backwards so he could face the candlemaker. "What about money? I could pay you for the information!"

"You have money?" Phillip lifted an eyebrow, disbelievingly. His hand tightened on the wooden pole and tried to ignore how much desperation was starting to leak into the merman's eyes. "I find that a little hard to believe, Pistol."

"Well, things equivalent to," Pistol said, waving his wrist around in a circle in the air. "You would not believe the stuff that gets thrown or lost down here that we scoop up and collect. Gold coins, gems, jewelry, name it and I'm sure I can get it."

"I see." Phillip continued walking. "That's very nice."

"No really, man. Try sunken cargo ships full of all that lovely stuff." Pistol was happy to note Phillip had stopped his march to stand and look at him. Progress was being made and that was good. Pistol should have thought of the money angle sooner; humans loved money. "I'm sure a pretty necklace might make the lady at home happy, am I right?"

"I doubt she'd condone murder for money." Phillip dropped the empty pole vertically, so that it rested on the ground and his shoulder. He crossed his arms and sighed. He couldn't be that much older than Pistol, unless there was some weird merman aging difference, but Phillip still felt like the boy's father. Phillip tried to be as calm as possible as he continued the conversation. If he reminded himself Pistol was a teenager, it might be easier to keep his cool during the negotiations he insisted on having. "I said we didn't get along, not that she was a bad person."

Pistol nearly growled, before controlling himself. That was okay. Everyone had their price, right? And he needed to get this Boris guy. Phillip was going to rat out his boss whether he liked it or not. Maybe if Pistol played his cards right he could even get Phillip to push the man in the water for him. Pistol bit his lip trying to think of what else to offer. Humans liked money and what else?

Pistol jerked straight up, smacking his stump into his other palm. "What about a girl?"

"A girl?" Phillip blushed slightly. There were only so many things a person could give a girl to another man for, and Phillip wasn't sure he liked where this conversation was headed. "What are you talking about?"

"A girl," Pistol said slowly, "to sleep with."

Pistol worried for Phillip if he didn't understand such a simple offer. This wasn't all that complicated. The guy had a kid so he had to know how this all worked! And he had a wife that gave him the cold shoulder all the time. Pistol raised his hand out of the water and waved it. How could he not understand the mechanics of this offer?

"I can get you one of those," Pistol said, waving his fingers in the air. "It'd be a great night out."

Phillip glowered at the merman, and picked up his pole. He moved on his way, shaking his head. Pistol had to be pulling his leg with that one. There was no other way Pistol could possibly think offering Phillip sex with some random girl would work. "Now you're just messing with me."

"No! Really! It'll be a girl from my neck of the woods and let me tell you that Sirens are the real deal. More beautiful than you can even imagine, and twice as fun in bed. Trust me when I say it can work just fine even if half of her is a fish tail." Pistol pushed forward in the water, right up to the edge of the road. This might be his ticket, because he hadn't heard an outright "no" yet. "And I know a few who owe me favors."

Phillip rubbed at his eyes. Pistol seemed to be forgetting something very important in this exchange. "I'm married. I have a three year old at home who might question why mommy is trying to kill daddy because he slept with a fish."

Pistol watched Phillip with the most serious expression he could muster. After a few beats, Pistol bit his lip and offered, "If fish isn't your thing, I know a chick who's half squid—"

"I'm going home." Phillip turned, face red as a beet, and his stride picked up speed. "You should do the same."

"Okay, so you don't want money or a good time," Pistol said desperately, watching his only real contact walk away. If he couldn't get the information from Phillip, he'd have to do a stake out at every pier and hope that the man wandered out onto it. Talking with the other humans wouldn't work because they'd turn him in to the boss again. Pistol was strong, but even he was at a disadvantage when ganged up on. Pistol pulled at his hair and was ashamed that he started whining. "What do you want?"

Phillip stopped again. Pistol looked down right needy with the pleading look on his face. The merman's eyes were wide and his sharp teeth were gritted together. Phillip squatted on the edge of the road and crossed his arms on his knees. "Look, I know that Boris is a horrible excuse for a human being, but I really can't help you kill him."

"I'm not hearing a 'why' in there." Pistol growled through his teeth. Only the need to hear what Phillip said next kept him from splashing the man with water or dragging him under again.

"Look, horrible human being or not, I have more than one reason to keep you from killing him." Phillip sucked in a breath and rubbed his face. He leaned over the edge of the river, and did his best to talk common sense into Pistol. "Even if we decided to push the ethics of murder aside, this entire town would basically go under if something happened to him. He owns the fishery, which employs over eighty percent of the population on this island.

"I even work for him." Phillip stressed this last bit by sticking a hand in his hair and pulling. Pistol kept his mouth shut, and Phillip sighed in relief that something must have gotten through to his merman skull. "Besides, if someone bumps him off, his second and third in command are just as cruel as he is but dumber than bricks. Who knows what they'd do to destroy the island if they were left in charge. At least Boris knows how to do business with the neighboring islands, even if he does employ illegal tactics to keep his power."

Pistol flicked his tail, causing a loud splash of water. Even he had to admit that was a slightly better reason for not killing the man than "It's wrong." Pistol thought back on the leader of his own clan and winced. He could probably relate to Phillip more than he'd like to admit. Slate wasn't exactly a picnic to serve under, either, but he was definitely necessary for peace with neighboring groups. Pistol rubbed at the brass covering on his stump, unaware that he was doing so. "The evil you know is better than the one you don't?"

"Yeah," Phillip said. His smile was sad, and he almost felt bad for Pistol. "That about sums it up."

"Well, I gotta' do something," Pistol growled through his teeth. He looked up at Phillip, eyes burning. "I'm a laughing stock down here!"

"To who?" Phillip asked.

Pistol shut his trap. He wasn't quite ready to start talking about his home life with a human just yet. Even if he was turning out to be an okay guy, cooperation or not. Pistol lowered slowly until only his head was above the surface of the water. "Nothing. Never mind."

Phillip watched as Pistol dropped under the surface and disappeared.

He sympathized with the merman's situation, but his hands were tied. This was probably a good lesson for the merman, when he thought about it. Pistol had a lot of pride, and where there was pride there was a fall, or maybe in Pistol's case, drowning. Phillip hoped he wised up: Revenge wouldn't help as much as he seemed convinced it would.

Phillip glared down at the surface of the water and the merman grinning at him. The feeling of déjà vu was overwhelming; Phillip's upper cheek twitched. It hadn't even been twelve hours and Pistol was already back and bothering him.

"I believe you tried this argument yesterday." Phillip covered his eyes, rubbing at his temples with his thumb and forefinger. Pistol had to be stalking him, or something, otherwise there was no other explanation for why the merman knew exactly when Phillip went to work. Never mind how Pistol managed to do that from the ocean or in under a few days. "And you came to the conclusion that I'd rather not risk a greater evil than my boss controlling the island."

"Yeah," Pistol said, eyes open wide and lip quirked in a tiny smile. He hid his teeth best as he was able, and tried to scrunch his shoulders up in an innocent pose. "But I thought it over and came to the conclusion that saving my pride is more important than any "what if's" when it comes to your town."

Pistol's quirky smile widened into a straight out grin, as if he had been right all along. The smug expression showed off every single one of his pointed teeth. Phillip lowered his hand and wrapped it around his own shark's tooth. He gripped it tightly and willed it to give him strength. "I'm sorry, but I have to disagree."

"I knew you would, which is why I've upped the ante." Pistol curled his finger back and forth toward himself, beckoning Phillip closer to the edge. Phillip stayed put, already knowing this trick. Pistol huffed; the man was learning. How was Pistol supposed to put them on even "ground" now? "I thought over my proposal yesterday and realized that you probably didn't accept because you couldn't wrap your mind around what I was offering!"

Phillip crossed his arms, still fingering the edge of the necklace. "That so?"

"Yes, which is why I invited a lovely siren to come say hello in person!"

Pistol raised both of his arms out of the water and held them out openly. If this didn't turn Phillip into putty in his claws, nothing would.

"Look, I already explained that I'm—" Phillip's voice caught in his throat. A second head rose from the water, like a goddess descending from the heavens in reverse.

The waters parted around her crowned head in shimmering droplets that looked like diamonds in the light. Phillip thought he was dead for the second time in his life. The head belonged to a woman—a beautiful woman—which was connected to an equally fair upper body. The bottom half remained hidden beneath the waves, but Phillip was too distracted by what he could see to even think about looking down through the murky green water for the other half. Her hair was golden, looking like it had been spun by Rumpelstiltskin himself for the miller's daughter. The sun glinted over it, reflecting the metallic sheen, as he watched it trail down to cover her naked breasts. Her eyes were as blue as sapphires, and Phillip was half convinced they were sapphires by the way they glittered.

Phillip swallowed, brain finally catching up with his mouth. "… married."

The siren giggled, voice sounding like a bell. Phillip was now well aware why sailors would jump from boats at the sound of their voice. She turned to Pistol with a nod, shifting her hair free to expose one of her breasts. Phillip's knees buckled, but his legs managed to keep the candlemaker on his feet.

Pistol grinned and looked up at the dumb struck man with his mouth hanging open. The merman wished he were high enough to smack Phillip's open jaw back into place. He knew this was the ticket. Pistol smirked, "You see? Totally worth it, and for a little information on your part, this lovely siren is willing to spend one—"

The siren grabbed Pistol's shoulder and dragged his pointed ear down to her mouth. Phillip tried not to stare as her lips whispered something to Pistol. *I'm a married man. I'm a married man. I'm a married man.* Phillip's mantra wasn't helping—she was still a vision of untouchable beauty and available for the low, low price of ratting out his snake of a boss.

Phillip pulled the top button of his collar loose and kept repeating his mantra.

"Man, you are one lucky guy!" Pistol grinned, smacking his hand on the surface of the water. He knew this was a good idea. "As it turns out, my siren friend here, Stygian, thinks you're cute. She's willing to spend not one, but two nights with you in exchange for more info."

Pistol glanced at the grinning girl and couldn't help the smirk. He mock whispered behind his hand, "I bet you can get even more if you play your cards right."

Phillip almost felt for his pulse as his heart picked up pace. The thought was in his head before he could stop it. Him and the siren, kissing on a rock as the sun set. Her delicate fish tail, dipping into the water, fins spread. Phillip knew it would be magical and he could even picture the moon rising as the sun dipped below the horizon.

Wife.

Phillip shook his head, clearing the image of the mermaid out of his mind. She was beautiful. She was straight out of a dream, but that didn't make it right. Phillip sucked in a breath, and whined like a child in his own head. *This is so not fair.* "I'm very sorry, but while she is absolutely gorgeous, she is not so much that I would cheat on my wife."

"What!?" Stygian snarled. Pistol cursed under his breath as the siren swam forward toward the shore. She ignored the merman and focused on the candlemaker. How dare that human! Stygian was a thousand times more beautiful than any human woman. This man was being offered heaven and he was turning it down because she wasn't pretty enough? Stygian's blood boiled and she set her targets straight for the ungrateful man who was going to *appreciate her offer dammit!* "I'm not *what?*"

Phillip backed away from the edge as far as he could go, until his back smacked into the wall of a shop along the river road. The woman lifted herself up to the shore edge, and he still couldn't see her lower half, but he prayed she wouldn't try crawling over. She could hurt herself! The siren hissed over the edge of the water and was holding herself up on arms extended straight. Phillip quickly turned his head to the left, so he wouldn't see her exposed breasts now that her hair had fallen down her back. "Ma'am, please don't be insult—"

Phillip yelped like his neighbor's dog after it had been kicked out of the house for eating the family dinner off the main table when something thick and heavy latched onto his leg and tugged.

Stygian dragged the man closer to the water, and wrapped her squid arm tightly around the man's waist. She lifted him off the ground and straight down into the water. "I'll show you who's not worth it."

Phillip coughed as her grip tightened, but he could now clearly see her lower half: She was half squid. She had eight, thick speckled auburn tentacle arms extending from the waist down, each covered with suction cups the size of his candle's wax catchers. Two much longer arms with thin flat triangular ends complete with their own suction cups ran on either side, one of which was wrapped around his waist. They were at least twice the length of her upper body, and it was now no surprise how she had reached Phillip from the river's edge.

Squid. Definitely squid.

A second arm squeezed around Phillip threatening to cut off his oxygen supply. It felt like his ribs were a second away from cracking in addition to irritating the wounds that Pistol had left days earlier. Phillip was more than a little worried they might open up again if she kept squeezing. Stygian rose out of the water, holding herself up on two stocky arms anchored in the shallow water to tower over him. She slammed two tentacles into the water, splashing his face.

Phillip begged, "Please."

"Shut up," Stygian said. The candlemaker closed his yap. She grabbed his face with her hand, pinching the chin. She forced him to look her in the eye. "Now tell me to my face that I'm not pretty enough to cheat on your dull little house wife with!"

"I think there has been a misunderstanding, Miss." Phillip gritted his teeth together, willing his lungs to pump oxygen under the stress. If he lived through this he was going to deck Pistol. "This is a matter of principle, not looks! I can't cheat on my wife! It would be wrong and unfair to her, no matter how gorgeous you might be!"

"She doesn't even like you," Pistol interjected. He tried to keep his body calm and relaxed, but he was keeping a close eye on Stygian in case she got out of hand. His childhood buddy had quite the temper when she didn't get what she wanted. Pistol had wanted her to seduce the candlemaker, not pop him like a cherry in her tentacles. "I don't see what the problem is."

"I'd be cheating on my wife!" Phillip shouted. He glared at the both of them. Was nothing sacred under the water? It must not be with all this talk of murder and cheating. They looked like people, but clearly they lived like animals. Phillip wondered if the anger wasn't clouding his thoughts, but that was not important at the moment! "That's the problem! I made a vow on my wedding day and I'm not breaking it, whether she loves me now or not!"

Stygian considered the candlemaker carefully. His heartbeat was racing so hard she could feel the pounding through his chest, clearly terrified of her might and power. She didn't think he was lying, though. Stygian could maybe give him a pass for declining her offer if his reason for passing her up was so honorable. Stygian pulled the man close enough that they were face to face. Her lips a breath away from his. "Is that the *only* reason you rejected my offer?"

"Yes!" Phillip shouted. He wasn't lying either. If he had been a man of lesser character, he would have most definitely caved to Pistol's demands upon seeing Stygian. Phillip shivered under that icy blue stare. Her lips were pursed in a frown, but Phillip couldn't help but notice she had a red lipstick of some sort. That or her lips were naturally the same red as an apple. "If I wasn't married, I'd take it in a heartbeat!"

"Fine." Stygian dropped the man in the water. He splashed about for a moment, coughing, and she shrugged. Stygian flipped her hair over her shoulder, showing off her impressive endowments. The candlemaker blushed, ducking his hair to stare at the water. He caught her reflection and turned his head to stare at Pistol instead. Stygian smirked.

"Your loss, honey," Stygian said, patting his cheek with the end of one of her tentacles. She turned to Pistol, expression changing in a flash. She was going to ream Pistol out for this later. She'd never been so embarrassed in her life. Stygian hissed in Pistol's face, "You owe me."

Pistol chuckled nervously as his friend swam off down the river back to the open ocean. He had a feeling it might be best to avoid Stygian for the next few days. There was a strange sensation niggling at the merman's back. Like a thousand suns were focused on a single point, determined to burn a hole in his skin. Pistol looked over at Phillip and realized those green eyes were the cause.

Pistol coughed into his hand and avoided eye contact. "I take it you're not convinced selling out your boss is the right way to go?"

"That was a siren?" Phillip asked steadily.

"Okay, so I lied about which girl I brought," Pistol shrugged, rubbing the back of his hair. He dropped his arms back in the water before looking at Phillip thoughtfully. "You can't blame me, though. Actually, you should probably be thankful I brought Stygian instead."

Phillip was briefly running through excuses of why he was going to show up to work soaking wet. "And why is that?"

"Because a siren would have eaten you afterwards."

Phillip buried his face in his hands and groaned.

Stygian had touched a nerve that Phillip had long forgotten. It had been over four years since Phillip had felt attraction to a woman—any woman. The way Stygian had affected him, was uncomfortable in more ways than one. Phillip reached into his shirt and pulled out his shark's tooth, holding it gently between two fingers. The sunlight set softly in the distance, coating the white surface in a tint of yellow. Stygian had brought back feelings and memories Phillip had buried for the sake of his peace of mind.

When Phillip was sixteen, he had fallen in love with the girl down the street. Her name was June, having been born in the same month of. She was his best friend and pretty in a plain sort of way with brunette hair and clear blue eyes. They were joined at the hip from the moment they met each other exploring the small forested areas on the edge of the island. Phillip could remember climbing trees, showing off his early apprenticeship skills in his master's workroom, and sharing a dessert of fresh strawberries in secret behind a rose bush.

She was the reason he stopped fantasizing about mermaids and sirens when he went to bed at night.

When he turned nineteen, Phillip had gathered every bit of courage he could to ask her father for June's hand in marriage. He gave his permission, and the arrangements were made. Their union was the last chance for the girl's family to carry on their line, as the father had no sons and his eldest daughter remained single. Her father was so happy about the wedding he arranged to have the dowry paid early to fund the house Phillip was going to build.

Everything was perfect until June died a week before the wedding from smallpox.

The dowry had already been spent on a new cottage, and Phillip had no way to return the money. A grieving and delirious Father decided that little house would not go to waste, and arranged for Phillip to marry his eldest daughter Sarah in place of his fiancé instead. Phillip's parents had agreed with June's father, and helped pushed him into the marriage offer. The arrangement was made in what felt like the length of a blink. Things had moved so quickly on their own, and they were made worse by Phillip's mind stuck in a daze from the grieving. Sarah herself, in much the same predicament, had very little to say over the issue.

In the end, Phillip walked his new bride down the aisle with a broken heart.

But years pass, and people learn to live with each other. Sarah hadn't liked the situation any more than Phillip had, but she also knew the wedding had been important to both of their families. At twenty-seven, there was a good chance this was Sarah's only chance at finding a husband, and neither Phillip's nor her own family were going to let her forget it. In the end, their child Icarus had been vital in keeping both Phillip and Sarah's sanity, even if his creation was less than pleasurable.

Each attempt had been awkward, fast, and any attempts on Phillip's part to make the process more bearable were met with a pillow to the face. After Icarus' birth, intimate relations of any sort had come to a resounding and welcome halt.

"Stop staring out the window," Sarah huffed, bringing Phillip out of whatever day dream he had been having. She cleaned her iron pot out with a scrub brush and watched as her boy tried to climb into his daddy's lap. "Icarus is trying to get your attention."

"Well, hello there," Phillip said softly, lifting his son up. He kept his arms around the tiny boy's waist and hitched him up higher on his lap. Icarus squirmed and reached for the curtains. Phillip held him up higher. "Did you want to see out the window?"

"Wet!" Icarus pointed out the window at a point in the distance. "Wet! Wet! Wet!"

"Yes, you can see the water all the way out there, can't you?" Phillip grinned, staring out his tiny square window. Five blocks down was one of the four edges of the island. Two entrances to the water involved straight drop offs from cliffs covered in trees, but the other two were soft sandy beaches. Phillip was lucky enough to live near one of the beaches. "Isn't it pretty?"

"Yes." Icarus tapped on the window with his finger. "Pretty."

Phillip smiled as he held his boy in his lap. He kissed Icarus on the side of the head and pulled the curtains over wider so he could see more of the ocean. However things had turned out with June and Sarah, at least this one particular end result was more than worth it.

CHAPTER 5

STAKE OUTS WERE overrated. Pistol huffed, nose just above the water as he hung around the rotting dock. The water was cold, the sun was setting, and it was clear Phillip was going to remain uncooperative. Without the candlemaker's help, Pistol would just have to get the information he needed all by his lonesome.

So far, he knew that the fishery had access to three of the major docks on the island that led straight out into the open water. One dock was attached next to the large gate of the pen he had been trapped inside, while the other two were open to boats on the perpendicular of the building. Whether or not Boris made rounds on those docks, was another matter.

He had a feeling that Phillip's boss might not be as hands on as Slate when it came to keeping track of his inferiors.

But, if Pistol could find Boris, he could follow the man home. His eyesight was far superior to any human's at night, and there were plenty of roads near the edge of the water. And if not there, Pistol could follow along on the main river. If the man was as rich and powerful as Phillip implied, than Pistol had no qualms assuming the man lived on the water. Pistol had never seen a wealthy human on an island pass up water front property. It was just how things worked up there.

"This sucks," Pistol hissed to himself as he slunk deeper below the surface. He snorted in the water, causing the space above his head to ripple. Watching from under the surface was a strain on his eyes, but it was better than having his redhead spotted. Pistol did *not* need to get captured again before he could track down Boris. Worst of all, he only had seen dock hands and other meaningless peons walking about. "This sucks!"

Pistol needed Phillip to do this, but that man was dead set on avoiding any involvement. That stupid candlemaker owed his life to Pistol. Sort of. That didn't matter. Phillip should still be far more eager to help take that fat idiot down than holding to his stupid ethical decisions. Pistol swam a circle around a dock post. On the other hand, Phillip was the first Pistol had met willing to save someone he feared, least of all at the potential cost of his own life. Phillip was unique; Pistol would give him that.

But way too much of a goody-goody for his own good.

Pistol shivered, remember Stygian's vengeance for her hurt pride. She had hunted Pistol down, threatened to strangle him if he didn't compensate her in some way for the embarrassment and her hurt pride. Pistol ended up having to give her a third of his treasure collection. A full third! And she took all the good stuff, too. Pistol would have to sneak back the ruby necklace and the tiara at a later date. Or at least beg for them back. Stygian was the type to take things as punishment and then give it back later when she felt bad for overreacting. Which was a plus for her character, and probably why they stayed friends. Stygian could only hold up the fire and brimstone anger for short bursts.

Still nothing compared to Phillip, who wouldn't have even taken anything in the first place.

Even with Pistol throwing it at him! The merman hit his head soundly on the wooden pole, shaking the dock about a millimeter. Thinking about Phillip made his head hurt. Pistol really should have just eaten him after he had escaped.

He thought back on wide, transparent green eyes and a little boy calling for his daddy from the road. The kid had been cute, and Phillip had changed when the kid showed up: He went into total parental protection mode, visible only by a slight shift in the tensing of his shoulders and the look in his eyes. Pistol pushed out from under the dock and looked up through the water. Or maybe it was best that he hadn't eaten the guy.

Phillip probably tasted horrible anyway.

The merman glanced up at the dock edge one last time before he called it a night and just went home. Even evil mob bosses got their sleep at night—or not! Pistol grinned like a lunatic when he saw *him* start to walk to the dock edge. Pistol swam closer, but stayed low merging with the shadows, to double check his target. A closer look at that ratty hair and plump face confirmed all he needed to know.

Boris cornered a large, meaty dock hand and started to yell at him. If Pistol had been paying the slightest bit of attention, he would have noticed that the dock hand was the same man who had thrown Phillip into the water. This probably would have registered as significant in that case. However, the merman wasn't paying attention to the conversation. His lids had already closed the black membrane over his eyes, he licked his lips, and Pistol could only think of one thing:

Target set.

"Alright, seriously!" Sarah said, keeping her voice low, but as stern as she was able. Icarus had been put to bed in the back room, snuggled neatly in the middle of their single straw mattress. Icarus slept in the middle so Sarah and Phillip could keep a proper distance, without either having to result to sleeping on the floor. It worked out well, and now that their little boy was asleep, Sarah could properly have a discussion with her so-called husband. She crossed her arms over her pressed apron and glared down at the overly distracted man. "What is going on with you?"

"What do you mean?" Phillip asked cautiously, pulling his shirt out from his pants. The sun had set behind the water a few hours ago, and Phillip was ready to hit the hay. He reached up to the candle sitting in the window and pinched the flame out. Pale moonlight filtered in through the window, lighting the room enough for their conversation. "Nothing's going on."

"No, you've been weird ever since you came home from work. What is it?" Sarah moved to block Phillip's path to the back bedroom. He wasn't going to get away that easy. "What happened? Did you meet that shark again?"

"Yes," Phillip admitted. "I saw Pistol. He's been very persistent about getting my attention lately."

"I thought you told him 'no' to that whole kill Boris thing?" Sarah asked. She rubbed her temple with a single hand, drawing little circles switching from one finger to the next. Her thumb dug into the side of her head last, relieving a bit of the pressure. "I swear, if that shark doesn't kill you, I'm going to with all the trouble he brings you."

"I did tell him no!" Phillip argued. The man walked across the small home and snipped out the remaining candle. The wax was low and melting around the wooden frame. Maybe he had been too distracted lately. Phillip picked at the glop of dried wax and tried to pull it from the sill edge. "He tried to bribe me again, that's all. And maybe this time he brought the bribe with him to try and tempt me in person."

"With what?" Sarah untied the back of her apron while keeping her eyes on her husband. It was pretty obvious now that Phillip's odd mood was related to that stupid shark he rescued. Sarah wondered how long this was going to continue before he came to his senses. "Gems or jewelry or something?"

"Something is right," Phillip said taking the apron after Sarah handed it to him, leaving the picked bit of wax for another day. He folded it neatly while she turned his back to him. Helping Sarah undo her corset was something he'd gotten used to over the years. June and Sarah used to help each other undress from these things before bed, but with her baby sister gone, that chore now fell to Phillip. He undid the strings mechanically and practiced. "He definitely got creative."

"Well, what was it?" Sarah pulled her hair down. Icarus was a light sleeper, so they had to change for bed in the main room of the house next to the fire and the kitchen table, as to not disturb him. The bedroom door was a good barrier as long as they were quiet. He still tended to wake when they snuck in, but he would soon sleep again when they curled around him. Sarah opened the chest on the far wall to pull out her nightgown. It would be nice if they had one extra room on the house to store their clothes or give Icarus his own room, but Sarah supposed two rooms in a home wasn't bad. The family down the block only had one room in the entire house with their mattress shoved in the far corner near the fire pit. "You still haven't said."

"It's not important," Phillip said. He moved the shark's tooth around his fingers, tugging on the leather strap. Phillip rubbed the smooth edge like a worry-stone, hoping he wouldn't rub it down to nothing in time. "I just fell in the water again."

"You're lying." Sarah turned around, blue eyes flashing. "What did he bribe you with?"

Phillip swallowed, Adam's apple bobbing in his throat. Phillip wasn't sure if Sarah would be angry or not. She only slept with him so many years ago for the sake of having children, and he honestly had no clue what her thoughts on Phillip seeking other company could be. Sarah might not even care at all that he had been propositioned. Phillip found it somewhat depressing he'd rather have her angry and hitting him than not care at all.

Phillip bit the edge of his lip and admitted, "A woman."

Sarah watched Phillip's face closely. His cheeks were turning a rosy shade of red and his eyes were averted to the floor. Sarah propped her hands on the sides of her dress. The edge of her mouth quirked in barely contained amusement. He couldn't be serious. Sarah tilted her head, and watched him closely. "For sex, right? He offered you a woman to sleep with?"

"Yes!" Phillip said, the word escaping his mouth before he could help it. The following words stumbled into a breathless slur. "Her name was Stygian and she was really pret—I, no."

Phillip covered his mouth. He took a deep breath through his hand, smelling the salt and sweat, before dropping it. "I may have been rather tempted."

Sarah laughed; full belly laughter complete with knee shaking. She didn't even try to keep her voice low: she just kept guffawing, bent over at the hip as she held onto her stomach. Sarah thought she was going to burst into a thousand giggling pieces if this kept up. Phillip looked strangled by her reaction; she laughed even harder.

Phillip bristled, clenching his fists. "What's so funny about that?"

"Like you'd say yes," Sarah said through the heavy breathing. She wiped the side of her eyes with the base of her palm, wiping away the tears. "Oh, oh I needed that."

"It's not that funny." Phillip huffed, throwing her corset into the clothing trunk. He didn't bother to fold it.

"At least she was pretty, right? Got yourself a good eyeful I bet." Sarah smirked, pulling off her overdress. She shook the dull brown garment in front of her and looked it over. It could go another day or two before it needed a wash. "Where'd he find a girl, anyway?"

"He has connections apparently." Phillip dropped his trousers and folded them. He picked up his own night clothes and swapped it for his shirt. "And she was an exceptionally beautiful mermaid, I'll have you know. Very exotic."

Phillip kept the fact she was half squid to himself.

Sarah snorted, rolling her eyes. "I'm sure you were horribly tempted."

"I might have been, considering she even came topless." Phillip said, unsure why he even brought that up. He ran his hand through his hair and dared to ask, "And what if I had taken him up on his offer? What if I had gone off for a night with a mermaid. Then what?"

"I would have congratulated you," Sarah said through a yawn. She smacked him on the shoulder and shook her head with one last laugh. "I'm going to sleep."

Phillip followed without answer. The sight of his little boy fast asleep on the bed soothed his confusing thoughts. Phillip slipped onto his side of the mattress and brushed bits of blonde hair out of his son's eyes, watching the chest rise and fall. He'd forget all about this in the morning.

All of it. Stygian and his laughing wife, both.

Pistol cursed when the path he followed ended near a beach outlet. The merman had been following his target for at least twenty minutes now, but he turned down an inland path where Pistol couldn't follow a few moments ago. He watched the man head toward a small group of cottages in the grass on the other side of the beach's sandy shore. They were tiny and made of mud and straw, which was hardly something a man of wealth would voluntarily live in. Pistol knew that much at least. He scrunched his nose, watching the chubby man walk up a path to one of the houses. *What would he be doing here?*

Pistol had to squint, but he still had a decent view of the house where Boris stopped from the beach outlet. He hid beneath the poles of a long dock sticking out from the beach in line with Boris' destination. The small lantern still burning on the outside of the house helped as well, giving that extra boost of light needed to focus. Pistol noticed the cottage was slightly larger than the surrounding homes, and was blessed with a thatched roof. In the window, he could only see darkness, and assumed that the occupants were probably asleep.

Pistol watched the proceedings with a curious eye.

Boris banged on the doorway with his thick, meaty fist, the hairs on the back thick like fur and bunched up at the sleeves of his jacket. When there was no answer, Boris pounded on the door even louder, this time accompanied by a direct order. "Chisholm! Open up!"

There was a slight crash from the other side of the door, a metallic ringing—a pot had knocked over? Boris could hear footsteps through the clatter and the door swung open quickly by the candlemaker he had come to visit. The man was thrown together, shirt untucked and trousers untied. Phillip Chisholm held his pants up with one hand, and his blonde hair stuck out in various directions. The candlemaker's breathing was heavy, and hands shaking.

Boris smiled. He loved it when he dragged people out of bed. Humans were always at their rawest form when they'd been denied a full night's sleep.

"Sir," Phillip said, heart beating a mile a minute. Boris was standing outside his door at the middle of the night. The man had a predatory smirk on his face, and all Phillip could think of was his wife holding Icarus tightly in the back room with a hand over his mouth to keep the boy quiet. The pounding on the door had woken them all, and there had been no mistaking who their visitor was. Phillip had a feeling his free and easy ride had ended. "Wh-what can I do for you?"

Boris rubbed his fingertips together, and leaned on the man's door. His presence forced the candlemaker to take a few steps back. "I had a little chat today with Mark, you see."

It's over, Phillip thought to himself instantly. He was a dead man. Plain and simple. Death by Boris' pistol. *Pistol.* Phillip nearly giggled at the absurdity of it all and the possible irony of that thought. He cleared his throat, "Was there a problem?"

"Well, that depends," Boris said, "on whether or not Mark was telling the truth."

Phillip felt his face flush with nerves. "What did Mark say?"

"I was yelling at him for working in the dark, you see, 'We have an in-house candlemaker for a reason!' I said." Boris rubbed his middle finger nail with his thumb. "But it seems at the mention of your name, he froze up in fright. I questioned him, but he refused to answer."

Boris leaned down in Chisholm's face. "He was too terrified of you to do as I asked."

"Was he?" Phillip's voice cracked.

"Yes, do you know what that means?"

"No."

"It means…" Boris trailed off, before dropping his hand on Chisholm's shoulder. He got down in the man's face, and the scrawny candlemaker started to breathe heavier. Their breath mingled in the chill air, Chisholm's crisp, and Boris' muggy. "You've been holding out on me."

"I'm so, so sorry—wait, what?" Phillip blinked.

Boris laughed and slammed down on the candlemaker's shoulder again, with a hearty laugh. "You've been holding back, haven't ya'? Who knew you had it in you to rough up Mark that way? I don't know what you did, but it worked."

"I…sir?"

"So here's what's what, next time I have a little problem or guy out of line? I'm coming to you. No more secrets now, boy! I'm on to you."

Phillip felt faint. "Right."

"Good lad," Boris said. He patted the man once more on the shoulder and walked back down the path humming. *And the candlemaker thought he could hide his other skill set from me,* Boris thought to himself. He turned and pointed straight at the candlemaker's face. "You can't hide things from me, kid! Don't you ever forget that."

Pistol couldn't hear the conversation from where he was at on the shore, but he could see when the target started to walk away. He was prepared to start swimming along the beach to follow when he glanced at Phillip. The second Boris hit the bottom of the hill and out of sight, Phillip dropped to his knees and held himself up by leaning on the doorway. His face was frozen in a horrified expression.

Pistol spent so much time concentrating on the candlemaker hyperventilating, that he lost track of the target. He smacked his stump into the water, the splash hitting himself in the face. "Shit."

CHAPTER 6

PHILLIP WALKED BACK and forth, thumb between his teeth along the edge of the pier. His box of spare supplies sat next to him on the ground, wax softening in the sun. For his personal sales and business, Phillip had to make the candles in his kitchen. But for official fishery work, he had a workroom fully stocked attached to the back end of the main building. Carrying supplies back and forth was a bit of a pain, but it was better than getting caught doing personal work on Boris' time.

Not that it had mattered in the end.

Phillip had made it halfway to work lugging the thing before his nerves caught up with him and he dropped the box on the side of the road to begin pacing. How on earth was he going to deal with work? It had been impossible enough to go back to sleep after Boris' visit, let alone prep properly for the day. Sarah convinced herself Phillip was going to get himself killed once the boss found out it was all a hoax. Phillip agreed with this statement. He had no idea how he got into these messes, or what he could possibly be expected to do about it. Phillip almost wished Pistol would show up to distract him.

"Mr. Candlemaker!"

Phillip stopped in his pacing, and turned to see Mark running down the street. "M-mark!"

"Boris just told me the news!" Mark exclaimed. He lived in a hut just down the street from their boss, so Mark made note to visit him every morning to see if there was anything that he needed. And this morning's visit had nothing but good news! "I'm so glad we're not in trouble."

"Right, not in trouble," Phillip repeated back. Mark was grinning at him. *Something is wrong here.* Phillip put his hands together in front of him, and put on a friendly smile. He pretended Mark was little Icarus after he had done something wrong, but was still inexplicably proud for having done it. "What exactly did he tell you?"

"That you're my new boss!" Mark grinned. He held his hands in fists and moved them up and down. "He said you're the new head of his 'heavy lifting' division. Isn't that great?"

"And what did you tell him to give me such," Phillip thought long and hard for a moment considering the right thing to say, "an honor?"

"Oh, that you were tough as nails and I seen 'ya wrestle a jungle cat!" Mark slapped the candlemaker's back, sending him stumbling forward.

"A jungle cat." Phillip righted himself and stared at Mark. People shouldn't be allowed to be that stupid. He rubbed his face, covering his mouth. "A jungle cat on our island?"

"Yeah! That was the best thing I could think of to explain the scars on your chest!" Mark smiled, proud of himself. Jungle cats were big and fierce and had claws just like the water beast. It was fool proof! "He's gonna' see them."

"That's, that's really great, Mark," Phillip said, feeling rather faint. He dragged his hand down his face and dropped it along his side. At least Mark had kept the merman a secret, but with that excuse Boris was sure to notice something was up. "We should get to work, then? Right?"

"Yeah!" Mark cracked his knuckles before trotting off ahead of the candlemaker to the main docks. He had a lot of product to move before the real "heavy lifting" could start that afternoon. "It's going to be fun watching you shove some people around!"

Phillip swallowed as he leant over to pick up his box of supplies and follow Mark along the road to work. This was not going to be a good day.

Not at all.

Phillip had been correct in his assumption.

His box of tools lay scattered on the ground where he had dropped them. Seconds after entering his work shop, two gorilla-like behemoths in worn trousers grabbed him by the arms, one to each side. Boris' "Heavy Lifting" crew at their best. They dragged him through the worn, open hallways of the fishery to Boris' main office near the edge of the docks.

They dropped Phillip at the front desk, literally, complete with a shove in-between his shoulder blades. His face smacked into the crooked floorboards, the pain exploding on his right cheek. Boris sat in his hard-back chair, lined with plush red cushioning. The luxury item looked out of place among the dilapidated wood and cracked windows, like a swan trying to fit in amongst a flock of deranged ducks. The man grinned and waved his hand for the two guards to leave. Mark stayed behind blocking the door, and Phillip shoved himself up.

Boris watched the candlemaker stumble to his feet. *No one pulls one over on me, candlemaker.* "Mark, did you tell him what I told you to?"

"Yes, sir! I did."

"Wonderful." Boris addressed the young Chisholm. "How are you doing?"

"Well," Phillip said, palms sweating against his pants. "Sir."

"Mark, do me a favor and remove the nice candlemaker's shirt, would you?" Boris asked innocently as a mosquito.

Phillip yelped as Mark dropped heavy fists around his waistline and yanked up, pulling the fabric up over his head. Phillip's limbs tangled in the fabric and he struggled to right himself as the brute undressed him. Boris' eyes were locked on Phillip's bandaged chest in a way that almost seemed indecent. Phillip's hand darted up to cover the shark tooth hanging around his neck. "Sir! What is this about?"

"The bandages, too. I want to see this scar you blurted about this morning, Mark." Boris tapped his hands on the desk. The candlemaker was going to pay for making Boris think he might have an intelligent muscle on staff. Then he had to go and dash poor Boris' hopes by being just lucky and a good escapist. Mark dutifully removed the wrappings from the man's chest, ripping at the yellowed fabric.

The scar under the bandages was red and swollen around the edges, the wound itself scabbed and ugly. Phillip resisted the urge to scratch at the scabs as they began to itch, exposed to the air and his goose bumps. That, however would only result in more bleeding. Phillip held his necklace to keep his hands occupied, tighter than he should have. The tip broke his skin, causing his hand to bleed. Phillip bit his lip as Boris looked at the incriminating injury. He held his tongue and waited for whatever judgment Boris decided true.

"Mark," Boris said, "where did he get that scar again?"

"A jungle cat." Mark nodded in confirmation. That part of the story he was sticking, too. After all, this was just a test to make sure the candlemaker had what it took to be on his crew.

"Alright, that's clearly a lie now that I've seen it," Boris said, pointing at the wound. "It's the wrong size. That there looks about the side of a human hand, doesn't it? Small cat would be smaller, and a jungle cat would be much larger, don't you think?"

"Oh," Mark said, eyes wide and blank. *Oops.*

"Where did he get it?" Boris asked, already with a good idea of the answer. "You must know, because whatever caused it scares you."

Mark looked between the two, and noticed that the candlemaker was shaking slightly. His eyes were wide and—Mark grinned. The candlemaker was scared of Boris! Well, that made things clear enough. Always stay on the good side of the scariest man in the room, that was Mark's philosophy. He answered, "The merman!"

No! Phillip screamed in his head. Out of the pan and into the fire. It dawned on him that he may never leave this room again. He had released Boris' prized possession and favorite pet. There was no more to it than that. Phillip turned his head to Boris, perfectly prepared to beg for his life. "Sir!"

"Shut up," Boris said, voice low and with an edge that could have rivaled the corner of the table top. "What do you mean 'the merman' did it?"

"I threw the candlemaker in the water when he was trying to let the creature go!" Mark said. He shrunk up against the door, lowering his shoulders as best he could. Curse his height! Made it impossible to shrink out of sight. Mark held his hands out. "But he beat it up and got out, so I was a little scared of him."

"You can go, Mark." Boris narrowed his eyes at the candlemaker. "Now."

Phillip watched as his only distraction ran from the room, leaving him alone with Boris.

"Now then, Chisholm," Boris said, adding a bit of sweetness to his voice. It worked about as well as trying to cover up the taste of vinegar with salt. "Let's you and I have a chat."

CHAPTER 7

PISTOL KILLED TIME slumped under the river dock he had previously used to stalk Phillip. A rowboat waiting for its owner knocked back and forth into the pier leg, creating a steady thumping that was oddly soothing. Pistol scratched at the barnacles clinging to the wood with his claws, forehead resting higher up. Boris' house was too far from the shore to be of any use, and he always traveled during high-traffic times on the roadway. Pistol attempted to make plans to catch the man on his few minutes near the water's edge while on the docks at work, but he couldn't focus.

Stupid candlemaker.

Pistol was worried about the idiot. There. He admitted it to himself as he dropped away from the pier and blew bubbles in the water. While nothing to Pistol, he could accept Boris was a legitimate threat to those endowed with flat claws and dull teeth. The man's visit with Phillip hadn't ended in blood and violence, but seeing the man fall to his knees like that struck Pistol's gut. Boris was going to do something to that human, and the merman needed more information.

Pistol smirked in the water. It might work two-fold, if Boris had indeed threatened the candlemaker it could work to both their advantage. Perhaps now the goody-goody would be on board with participating in his master plans to kill the fat lug. Surely Phillip had some sense of self-preservation in that head of his? Pistol hadn't nearly gotten to know the man as well as he'd like yet, so him getting himself killed wasn't an option. The merman could definitely see them being friends once this was all over.

Not that Pistol was lonely or anything.

No, no. It had nothing to do with that. Pistol ducked under the water when a woman carrying a basket full of eggs and a squirming chicken walked by the road. Sure, the majority of Pistol's Shiver was avoiding him at the moment due to the ever increasing bad blood between him and Slate, but that was inconsequential. It wasn't like hanging out with another guy was all that great or anything. Or that the candlemaker made him laugh.

Nope.

Pistol smacked his forehead into the wooden beam holding up the dock. The merman needed more friends. That's what he needed. Stygian just wasn't cutting it, and his next best option was a guy who made candles and used a shark's tooth as a good luck charm. Pistol wondered where down the road he had gotten this desperate for company?

Phillip turned the corner around a side shop, placing him on the main road along the river. Pistol's self doubts were lost, evaporating like a puff of smoke. Like a puppy, he darted over in the water around the row boat and pulled himself up on the side of the walk. "Phillip!"

Phillip spotted Pistol in the river, the grin on his face revealing his rows of pearly teeth. He held himself up on the shore via an elbow and a hand, leaning on one side. One of his pectoral fins was flattened in an odd angle on that side, and Phillip wondered if that hurt. Pistol didn't appear to notice, smiling and practically vibrating in place, so perhaps not. The tip of his caudal fin moved back and forth in the water, creating small ripples behind him.

Phillip wondered which type of shark's tail Pistol actually had. He knew that different sharks had different tails, but not enough to know which one. Maybe he could ask one day, assuming he got the chance.

Phillip fingered the necklace around his neck, as he came to a stop between the merman and the crooked dock. He lowered himself down to sit next to Pistol in the dirt, letting his feet hang over the side of the drop to the river at the knee, shoes inches from the surface of the water. The merman crossed his arms in the dirt, and Phillip smiled. "Hello, Pistol."

"Finally giving into the inevitable, huh?" Pistol turned so that he faced the candlemaker. Phillip's shirt was un-tucked from his pants, and his work apron hung over his arm. The long waist strap dangled down, the tip getting wet in the water. Pistol reveled in the familiarity, but tensed all the same at the unusual behavior. "I notice there's no defiance or fighting to keep your distance, today."

"How did you lose your hand?" Phillip asked without preamble, looking at the stub resting next to him on the river's edge. The brass covering reflected the sunlight as Pistol moved, drawing attention to itself.

"What?" Pistol asked, holding his wrist up to look at it. He twisted it in the air, letting the evening sun reflect off the brass covering he'd spent two days making. Pistol watched Phillips face. The candlemaker looked drawn out and tired with heavy bags under his eyes; like he had seen something haunting. Pistol set the residual limb back on the edge of the road. "Why?"

"Just curious." Phillip moved his eyes back to the surface of the water. He chose to stare at Pistol's lower half instead, taking in the multiple fins and parts. There was a tear in his dorsal fin that lined up with a scar down the full side of his body. Pistol was covered in scars that Phillip hadn't taken the time to notice. "I'm sorry if it was intrusive."

"Not really." Pistol scrunched his face as he processed what Phillip had asked. Pistol didn't think he'd ever actually told someone what happened. Everyone else either already knew, or didn't care enough to ask. "It's just an odd question."

"Really?" Phillip slipped his necklace off his neck and held the charm in his hand, moving the tooth around in his fingers. This was nice, with the water splashing softly against the shore and the sun setting in the distance painting the area in red and orange. "Is it impolite to ask about scars?"

"Not impolite, just more no one bothers." Pistol rubbed the back of his head. He straightened his arm, pushing himself up on the river side to stand on his hand. Pistol waved the other arm in the air in a small circle. "Scars are scars, and everyone's got them. Some are from fights, others are from accidents, and whatever else. It's just not that big a deal."

"But that's not a scar," Phillip said, "your hand was amputated. That seems like a bigger deal. Or at least, it was when we realized my son's hand couldn't be saved."

Pistol dropped back down and crossed his arms on dirt road. Phillip's fingers twisted the cord of his necklace. "What happened to your kid's hand?"

"It was crushed under a box of tools that someone knocked on top of him. He broke two fingers, and the top of his knuckles were sliced open.

The doctors did what they could, but the wound got infected anyway." Phillip dropped the tooth, catching it by the end of the thread before it could fall in the water. "The dying flesh spread faster than he could heal. The doctor dropped the ultimatum that it was either cut it off or my son died. So, I guess to answer your question, I just figured amputations were in the extreme measures category, even for a merman."

Pistol pushed off the side and ducked into the water. He pulled himself up a moment later, skin dripping with excess water. "I mean, yeah it was bad enough that I had to get it cauterized to close the wound, but you really just want to know what happened?"

"Yes," Phillip answered. He wanted to know as much about the merman next to him as possible. It would make things easier in the long run. "If you don't mind, I'd like to know how you lost your hand."

"I took things one step too far with Slate," Pistol tapped his claws on the shore one at a time. "He lost his temper and off it went. Cut it clean off with a stone he'd sharpened."

Phillip's blood ran cold from Pistol's straight-to-the point, almost bored, explanation. He spoke as if the subject was Sarah throwing a spoon at his head, not the removal of a functional limb. No wonder Pistol was able to kill so easily. If having a hand chopped off by a fellow was just another day, than what was a few more bits cut off? Phillip licked his lips. "Slate?"

"Oh, Slate is my Shiver's leader," Pistol rubbed under his nose, before laughing suddenly. He rolled a bit in the water and shrugged. "He's got a trigger temper, but normally he just smacks me around a bit when I step out of line. I pushed the wrong button that day and he really let me have it."

Pistol was chuckling and Phillip's stomach lurched. How was that even remotely amusing? "What—what did you do, exactly?"

"You know?" Pistol cradled his head in his arms, eyes up on the human. "I don't even remember. I was like ten at the time, so it could have been anything. I should have known better, anyway, even as a pup. Inheriting the Shiver at seventeen had to be stressful for Slate, and he was already a pretty twitchy guy."

"I'm sorry," Phillip said.

My turn to ask a pointed question, Pistol thought to himself as the silence between himself and Phillip stretched on. "What did Boris say that's got you looking like someone raided your food stash? I saw him at your house the other night from the beach."

Phillip jerked; no point in hiding it. "The short version is that he knows I was the one who let you out."

Pistol hissed accordingly, smacking the shoreline with his stump hard enough to knock a clump of dirt loose into the water. He bit his lip, hissing as the sensitive nerves at the edge of his wrist whined from the mistreatment, but ignored them. "What'd he do?"

Phillip appreciated that Pistol understood the seriousness of the situation, but bit the edge of his lip all the same. "He also knows that I've met with you afterwards a few times since then."

Pistol pulled up higher to look the candlemaker in the eye. "How does he know that?"

"He knows I let you out because Mark is a simpleton." Phillip wrapped the cord around his finger, tooth hanging near the edge of his index.

"He knows we've met since then because I've recently discovered I sing like a canary under physical intimidation." Pistol was giving him a funny look, so Phillip clarified. "Boris got very creative with a lit candle, and we'll leave it at that."

Phillip rubbed fingers over the skin where Boris had dribbled the hot wax on his belly and back before shoving the lit end of the candle into his skin to snuff it out. Boris then had re-lit the candle and repeated the process. Over and over and over. To someone where amputation was an acceptable punishment for pestering, Pistol probably thought him pathetic. "I'm ashamed to say I only held out for twenty minutes."

"Yeah, that is a little short," Pistol agreed. He shook his head and tugged on the edge of Phillip's shirt sleeve. "So how'd you get off the hook for the you know, death, after the torture fun?"

"I had to make a deal."

"What deal?"

"Trick the merman into being captured again."

Pistol's body tensed, eyes immediately searching the area for some sort of ambush. His nose opened, but he couldn't smell anything outside the ordinary aside from the odd waxy smell that clung to Phillip's skin and clothes. Pistol kept his eyes darting from spot to spot as he talked. He would *not* be caught again. "You telling me that as a warning, or because it's too late to matter?"

"Warning," Phillip said. He tapped the back of his ankle against the dirt bank, watching the water. Phillip felt oddly calm for a man who could very much be dead by tomorrow. "I was on my way home to get my wife and kid on a boat before Boris could think to involve them."

"Not getting on that boat yourself?" Pistol asked.

"Then he'd definitely be interested in getting them involved. Low tolerance for pain or not, I'd prefer his wrath stay focused on a single target, thank you." Phillip dropped his necklace back around his neck. The tooth bounced against his freshly bandaged chest and fell back into its proper place. Bits of candle wax clung to the scaring from Pistol's wound under the wrappings that he needed to clean out when he back home. "Even Boris wouldn't blame me for shipping the family out."

"So, what? You're giving up?" Pistol yelled, shaking Phillip's arm. "What are you going to do? Go back tomorrow to say 'No can do! The merman split 'cause I tipped him off! Have fun torturing me?' "

"Not quite." Phillip tapped the crown of the scowling merman's hair with the back of his knuckles. "I was going to ask if you had an idea to help get me out of this mess, but now I'm reconsidering."

Pistol smirked, showing off his teeth. He patted Phillip's chest with his wrist, the brass covering clicking against the man's shark tooth necklace. "Oh ye of little faith, not only do I have a high tolerance for pain, but I'm also rather crafty, if I do say so myself. I think I can solve your little problem for you."

"Oh?"

"For a price, of course."

"I figured," Phillip rubbed the back of his head. "But what do I have to lose at this point?"

"Glad you see things my way." Pistol grabbed the top edge of Phillip's shoulder sleeve to pull his head down near his own. Pistol whispered conspiratorially in Phillip's ear: "This is what we're going to do."

CHAPTER 8

"WHY ARE YOU packing me up to stick on a boat, again?" Sarah asked, rubbing her back just above the apron tie. The sun had almost disappeared on the horizon and her husband was acting weirder than usual. Phillip studiously packed and folded her belongings in their clothing chest, items of value neatly tucked between the folds. "Because normally we're packing up for bed right now."

"I'm an idiot, that's why." Phillip grabbed Icarus' few toys and sat them alongside his wife's books in the corner of the trunk. His own clothes sat folded on the outside, removed to make room for his wife and child's things. Phillip loaded chunks of cheese and salted meat wrapped in paper into the other corner. It should last them about a week, and the boat trip should only be a few days. "That's what you want to hear, right?"

"I want to know why you're shipping me and Icarus out to the sea in the middle of the night." Sarah pulled a chair out and sat down. She crossed her legs under the skirt and watched Phillip securely close the lid of the trunk. "Or the better question, how you think you can force me to go."

"Look, I pissed off Boris. He's out for blood and I'm about to make it worse. I would feel much more comfortable if you and Icarus were off the island for the next few days."

Sarah rubbed between her eyes. "The closest island is three days away assuming the weather stays good. It'd be a trip straight there and back."

"I know." Phillip rubbed the sweat from his forehead. He pulled off his shirt in one swift movement and pulled out a clean pair of clothes. Might as well change now; he wouldn't be sleeping tonight. "Boris has a short memory and that'll give you a few extra days for him to forget you exist."

"And you're not giving out specifics, because?" Sarah stood and walked behind her husband. His shoulders shook, but whether it was from nerves or excitement she hadn't quite figured out.

Probably both.

"It's complicated. If I'm still alive afterwards, I'll share." Phillip grabbed his apron as an afterthought, sticking a few of his sharper carving tools in the front pouch. It'd probably be good enough to take out an eye if worse came to worse. His hand to hand combat was useless, but he'd yet to meet someone who didn't flinch when a knife jabbed through their skin. Phillip tied the apron around his waist, securing it in the back and straightening the straps.

"I'm not going anywhere, Phillip."

He turned to face his wife, dropping his voice intentionally to avoid an argument. He didn't want to wake Icarus just yet. "Sarah, look—"

"You look here, Phillip." She smacked the front of his chest with the flat of her palm. He moved back an inch from the force. Sarah shifted her hand into a fist and punctuated each sentence with a hit to his chest. "I'm not my baby sister. I can handle myself. I don't need *you* to protect me."

Sarah tugged that shark tooth necklace out from Phillip's collar. She held it in her hand and tugged his head down using the strap to be level with hers. "Boris doesn't scare me, but more importantly, I trust you."

"Sarah?" Phillip asked, reaching up and touching her hand. She let go of his necklace and rubbed her hands on the bottom of her skirt. Phillip held the necklace in her place, squeezing it tight as she walked over to the trunk.

"Don't read too much into that. I said I trusted you, not had a change of heart. If anyone can get the best of Boris, it'll probably be you and that stupid merman." Sarah opened the chest and pulled out the cheese and meat. She was up, she'd made her self hungry with yelling, and it was already out of the cupboard. Midnight snack it was. Sarah slammed the lid down on the chest and sat on it. "So I'm not going anywhere. Go to bed, Phillip. I have a feeling you'll need the sleep."

"Sarah," Phillip said, his hand digging into his apron. He shook his head and sat next to her on the trunk. "I don't think I could sleep if I wanted to."

"That makes two of us," Sarah said, passing over a chunk of cheese wrapped in meat.

Phillip bit into it and prayed Pistol's plan worked.

Boris waited. The shadows of the alleyway covered his heavy form where he stood, the rolls of his back fat pressed flat against the mud wall. The candlemaker was to bring the merman with him to a small cove that outcropped from the side of the river. It was a popular fishing spot for the kids, but today it stood empty. Five men stationed around him in the alleys waited for his signal, ready and raring to go. At once they would jump out with nets and poles with loops around the end like the ones used to capture mad dogs.

They had all learned to keep their distance.

If all went as agreed, Chisholm would ask the merman to accompany him for a chat as he walked to the market. Once the merman was trapped in the inlet, his men would use nets to cut off his escape, and use the poles to restrain him. The candlemaker would be on his way to forgiveness, Boris far from done with the coward's punishment, and Boris would have his prize possession back. In a matter of hours, his complete status quo would be restored.

The sky turned orange, mixing in pinks and a few leftover blues here and there as he and his team waited. The candlemaker would arrive in a few moments, assuming he kept his word. Just light enough to see, but close enough to nightfall that the kiddies were safe at home in their beds.

Boris liked to do things the right way.

Chisholm rounded the bend, right on time. His gait was smooth, and his hands were in the pockets of his work apron. Boris tapped his fingers on his arm as he watched. Chisholm's smile was casual as he chatted to the water. The candlemaker was the picture perfect image of relaxation.

Good actor, Boris thought to himself. A splash in the water next to the candlemaker had a grin splitting his face. *Right on time.*

Boris saw the back fin of the shark-creature surface and go under. His heart beat sped up in his chest as the candlemaker and the monster came closer and closer to the trap laid for the merman. Every once in a while the monster's head would split the water, further proof that he'd almost captured his prize. Boris' fists tightened in excitement.

It had been quite some time since he had such a perfect killer under his "employ" and he was eager to get it back.

Chisholm walked around the inlet's edge, stopping at the center of the cove's defining arc. When the merman slipped into the shallow area to get a better view of the candlemaker, Boris struck the signal: A shout of "Get 'em!"

Men dashed out from every opening of every alley and hiding place with their poles and nets. The merman screeched and dived under the water, but Mark was faster. The bulky man hooked the loop around the merman's neck, allowing the rest to have an easier time grabbing his limbs and tail. The candlemaker shouted in protest, but was shoved aside to the ground. Mark watched someone kick him in the side for good measure.

The merman was captured in less than five minutes.

CHAPTER 9

STRUNG OUT, THE various leather straps attached to the long poles pulled Pistol in every direction. The one around his neck nearly choked him as it kept him high above the water. Pistol's entire torso was exposed to the air, as well as a few inches of his tail. One pole strap had been wrapped around his elbow, and another around his wrist on the other arm. His limbs were held apart as far as possible, stretched to their limits. One last pole had sunk into the water to grab his tail around the caudal fin. Pistol was going to be sure to bite the hand off whoever was pulling on the end of that particular pole.

And he wouldn't let them join the "one handed" club, either.

Because he'd kill them right after. And eat the rest of them. But those fantasies were best left for when Pistol wasn't hanging in the air like some sort of wild dog.

"Let me go!" Pistol shouted, pulling with all his might. A second and third loop appeared to restrain him further, snagging his neck and arm again from different angles. Phillip pulled at one of his captors, but was elbowed in the gut for his troubles. The candlemaker hit the ground, and someone began to kick the man while he was down. Pistol snarled, "Hey! Leave him alone!"

Boris sauntered up to the candlemaker and stood patiently as he waited for the goon to notice his presence and back off. His faithful man did, and scrambled away from the trouble making candlemaker. Boris watched the man struggle to his feet, his eyes alight with an angry fire. That was a good thing; passion. Now if only it wasn't so misplaced. Boris pat the candlemaker on the shoulder. "Good job."

"Good nothing," Phillip replied, voice rasp from the pain under his ribs. Not only had it hurt, but he was sure that Pistol's first wound had reopened *again*. Phillip held his hand over his ribs and squeezed. "Let him go, Boris."

"After all this work?" Boris pressed his fingers on the candlemaker's chest. He could feel the warm blood seeping through the bandages, and brought his fingers away wet as it soaked into his apron. Boris leaned forward, grinning in the man's face. "Unlikely."

"Get away from him!" Pistol shouted. A heavy shove sent Phillip splashing into the water next to Pistol. The gangly, pig-faced men laughed as he struggled to right himself in the shallow pool. Pistol growled at them all, tugging at his restraints again. "Hey! I said to leave him alone, you water rat!"

"That's an odd attitude to have," Boris remarked, stepping closer to the shore. The merman trembled with rage, angrier at the treatment of the candlemaker than himself. Boris smacked the monster in the face. The back of his palm came back red, covered in tiny scratches from scraping the merman's rough skin. The merman smirked, Boris kicked him in the gut. "After all, the candlemaker here just sold you out."

"Of course he did," The merman rasped, taking a moment to work through the shock to his intestines. As the overweight man's face dropped in confusion, Pistol sniggered in place, shaking his bonds. "You really think that idiot could lie to save his life?"

Boris rubbed his knuckle, smoothing out the reddened skin. "So you just let yourself be captured?"

"Yeah," Pistol said, "I thought it would be fun."

Boris studied the merman. His candlemaker friend waded toward the edge of the pool, gripping tightly to his wounded chest and hissing. The merman's face split in a toothy grin that seemed to take up the entire width of that ugly mug of his. The razor sharp teeth clashed together, showing off a second row behind and their serrated edges. Boris took a step back. "What fun?"

A splash of water lurched from the river, coating Boris and all of his men in a salty bath. Boris choked as he cleared his lungs. His men dropped their sticks from the force, and struggled to regain their holds.

"I think seeing the look on your faces right about now counts as fun," Pistol said, grabbing one of the poles that held his neck. Pistol ducked as a squid arm darted out from the water, wrapping itself around the the ankle of the poor goon who held the other end of the pole. The arm whipped back, pulling the goon into the deeper part of the river. Pistol pulled the loops from around his neck, and broke the sticks in his hand. "I think it's even funnier that you guys thought I'd be stupid enough to come alone."

Boris gaped as his men started to disappear into the water one by one, each grabbed by a thick, suction-cup ladened arm. They vanished below the surface almost too quickly to see what had grabbed them. "What is going on?"

In the meantime, Pistol took his chance and grabbed the lackey who had kicked Phillip. He shoved the man's face into the dirt lining the water, grinding his cheek there until it turned red. Pistol lifted the man's head and smashed it viciously into the surface over and over until blood poured from a broken nose. The intoxicating smell filled Pistol's nose, and he could feel his pupils hide behind the black membrane as it came out from the side of his eyes.

Pistol nearly took a bite.

The water splashed against his side as Phillip moved to the corner. Pistol watched the blond man for a full second before grinding his teeth. *Not the time.*

"You didn't honestly think I was the only one under water like me, did you?" Pistol dropped the man's face back into the dirt and held it there, amused by his coughing and frantic fingers flopping into the wet soil, desperate for purchase. "I'm a little insulted you think I have no friends."

"Pistol." Phillip said, a light hesitation in his voice. The boy's auburn eyes had disappeared behind inky black, a dire warning that things could get much uglier much faster than he'd hoped. Phillip saw Pistol's muscles tense, revealing the monster the candlemaker had nearly forgotten in his short, casual chats. The merman was going to suffocate that man at the rate he was going. "I think you need that guy up now."

Neither Pistol nor Boris chose to listen to Phillip, eyes on Stygian in her full glory, standing above the water.

Her beauty caused a momentary silence to fall over all watching, before her lips smirked. Phillip watched as the four of Boris' attendants not held captive by Pistol were lifted from the water with her much stronger lower half. They were screaming through the water they coughed up. Her eyes weren't black, but the expression was just as empty and icy.

The same dead emptiness all fish had seemed to master.

Phillip felt at this point, his little rescue mission had officially gotten out of hand.

The point was to scare Boris and the others into leaving them alone, but the look on both Pistol and Stygian's faces promised more. Flashbacks of blood and sharpened claws made themselves known in Phillip's head.

Had Phillip really forgotten the brutality and viciousness of Pistol from a few brief conversations? Pistol could rip a man apart, to eat them Phillip had to remind himself. And who knew what Stygian was truly capable of? She tried to rip him apart for not wanting to sleep with her!

There was an echoing of snaps, a chorus of broken bones as the squid-human hybrid closed her limbs tightly around the struggling men. Phillip looked away, covering his face and ears as the men screamed.

He felt sick.

"They ain't dead," Pistol snorted, knocking out the man he held on a rock. He lifted the goon by the back of his sopping wet shirt and threw him on shore, still breathing. Phillip shook in the water, head to toe, creating a series of ripples and miniature white-caps. Pistol dropped lower into the water, and huffed. "She just broke a few limbs."

Phillip hesitantly looked at the men swimming to shore, limping or holding their arms tightly to their chest. That was much better than the broken rips and crushed internal organs he had originally pictured hearing the breaking sounds. Not by much, but better. "That's, that's a relief."

"You're such a pansy," Pistol said. He bumped the man's back with his shoulder before turning to Stygian. He grinned up at her, enjoying the view of her exposed chest, her blonde hair cascading down her back instead of her front. "Nice job."

"You owe me another necklace," she said, before waving her fingers at the candlemaker. Stygian plopped herself down next to the edge where the candlemaker clutched the shore. He was just so adorable when he was terrified. Why did Pistol have all the luck? "Hello again, cutie."

"Hello, miss," Phillip said. He edged an inch closer to Pistol, hoping the squid didn't notice.

"And don't think I forgot about you," Stygian smiled, as she watched the heavy-set man try and slip away.

Boris didn't have time to run before he found himself tangled in the arms of the squid-woman. *She was on shore*, he thought absently as he shoved at her tentacles. Boris watched as she maneuvered herself closer, walking her fat limbs as they slid on the dirt. She slammed him into the ground by his arms and legs, limbs spread the same way the merman had been not a few moments earlier. "L-let me go!"

"I don't think so, sweetie," Stygian said. She pulled her hair over her chest, not wanting to grant the man beneath her any favors. She settled on the edge of the pool, pushing her upper arms aside. She maneuvered the man into a tightly wrapped bundle the way she had done a million times with any tuna or creature who crossed her. Stygian pulled the bundle in closer, her mouth watering. "But Pistol promised me a snack. He hates fatty foods you see, but I'm quite fond of them."

"What's she doing?" Phillip asked. They were behind Stygian, so he couldn't see what suddenly had Boris screaming and clawing at the ground. Phillip grabbed Pistol's shoulder and shook it. "What's she doing?"

"Oh, have you never seen a squid eat anything before? It's something else." Pistol draped his arm around Phillip's shoulder and pushed them both forward to see around Stygian's tentacles. "See? She's got a beak down there just like a regular squid. You should see her bite into a big old tuna fish!"

"What?" Phillip shouted. He turned again, this time clearly able to see the large beak under the moving tentacles. Boris inched closer to the opening, leg close to the tip of the bird-like beak peaking out of the flesh. Phillip shoved at the merman's chest. "Stop her! You said you weren't going to kill him!"

"I lied?" Pistol slumped against Phillip, hanging off his back like a pup. He wondered if there would be leftovers as he eyed the man's bulky form. He licked his lips. "And technically, she's killing him, not me."

"Make her stop!" Phillip said. The beak opened wide, revealing a soft tongue, and the sharp edge glinted in the lantern light. Boris' leg was dragged into the opening. Phillip had no doubt a single snap would take it right off.

Phillip yelled, "Stop her now!"

"Why? The guy's a jerk and you're better off without him. Changes in power aren't that big of a deal." Pistol grabbed Phillip when he started toward the shore. *Idiot.* Didn't this guy have any sense of self preservation? Pistol hissed in Phillip's ear, "Don't get in her way. You'll just make her mad."

"I need to stop her," Phillip said, voice hoarse as he fought against Pistol's hold. The brass covering on his stump hit Phillip in the jaw when the merman put his arms around his waist to hold Phillip back. He turned in Pistol's grip and pointed at the screaming man. Murderer or not, this wasn't right. "This is too far, Pistol! Now let me go! I need to do this!"

"No, you don't. Calm down." Pistol adjusted his grip on the man's waist to hold him in the pool and away from a feeding Stygian. *Where'd all this energy come from?* Phillip really needed to get over this killing thing. He was an omnivore, wasn't he? Pistol got elbowed in the face for his troubles. He dug his claws into the man's stomach and wound his other arm around his neck, finally holding Phillip still. "Would you settle down and let her eat him already!"

"Release me." Phillip said, voice calm even though his bleeding chest ached and everything hurt. He shoved his hand into Pistol's cheek, shoving him away and rubbing his palm raw on his rough skin.

"Would you two knock it off?" Stygian huffed. She dropped the sobbing man to the ground, losing her appetite as the two men behind her argued. The fat slob scrambled away, but she whipped him back with a loose tentacle. "It's really hard to keep up an appetite when you two are bickering like children back there."

"Ms. Stygian, I know he is an absolute waste of a human being, but I must insist that you let him go," Phillip said, Pistol still wrapped around his chest, holding him in the water. Phillip looked down at the man sobbing, arms covering his head as his lower half stayed wrapped in the tentacles. "I think he's learned his lesson about catching anything other than small fish."

"I don't know, I'm rather hungry," Stygian said, sitting upright and hiding her beak again beneath her. The air was cold, anyway. The squid hybrid slipped down into the water, wrapping her human arms around Phillip's shoulders from the front. Pistol didn't remove himself from the human's back, but that was fine. Stygian merely pressed up against him, wrapping her hands up behind his ears and on his neck. "What'll you give me instead?"

"I—" Phillip stopped. Her bare chest was flush with his own and Boris clawed at the shore in the background. Phillip found it quite difficult to think with her blue eyes staring into his own, and her gold hair tickling his cheek. He tried to edge away but was trapped in place with Pistol still at his back. "Nothing, but I would very much appreciate it either way."

Stygian chuckled and kissed the candlemaker on the lips. It was like kissing a rock, the man refusing to budge and kiss back. "I guess you win this one."

She threw the fat lard down the roadway, but not before snapping his leg below the knee. The man screamed out in pain, curling into a ball to hover his hands around the break.

Stygian turned back to the gasping Phillip. "You're lucky you're cute."

Stygian kissed Phillip on the cheek before disappearing below the water as quickly as she had arrived.

Phillip dragged himself from the water slowly after Stygian's leave. He left a sopping trail of water and mud as he crawled up the bank and shook himself off. He rubbed at his chest, wincing at the apron and shirt he'd have to replace as the blood stained the front. But, at least the bleeding had stopped. And it didn't hurt nearly as much as the hole Pistol drilled in his back with his glaring alone.

Phillip ignored him and walked over to Boris. "Sir?"

"What the hell do you want?" Boris said, scooting away from the pool as far as possible. He clutched his limbs tight to himself, the feeling of the creature's hot breath still clinging to his skin. Rough bruises from the suction cups itched on every exposed surface. "Isn't it bad enough that you sent your monsters on me? What more do you want!"

"Like you've got room to talk!" Pistol shouted from the sideline, the snarl in his voice a rumbling growl. *Guy should be squid-food by now!* Pistol slammed his hand on the water surface, splashing it up toward the fat man. "You're a thousand times worse than me and Stygian! At least when we kill people, we eat them!"

Boris pointed a finger, grateful the fish couldn't climb out of the pool. "You shut up! I preferred it when you were just a stupid animal!"

"Well that makes two of us!"

"Enough!" Phillip shouted loud enough to silence the two of them. The man untied his apron and squeezed the water from the fabric. He held it to his chest, and rubbed between his eyes. "Listen. Boris, you need to stop going after Pistol and his people."

"Why you ungrateful wretch." Boris stood, water plastering his hair to his eyes. He favored his good leg, the broken one sending strips of pain all the way up to his spine. "I'm in charge here!"

"Yeah, we can all see that." Pistol snorted from the shoreline. "Want me to call back Stygian? I'm sure she'd love to refute that."

"That won't be necessary," Phillip said, resolve steeling his voice. His insides shook like a wet cat, but his composure held. He only got one shot at this. "I'm asking this of you, Boris, because sending you away for good is a disagreeable option when I know who's going to replace you, and killing you is wrong no matter what sort of a horrible human being you are."

Phillip rubbed his stomach where the wax burns still lingered. Boris had the sense to flinch, remembering the action. Pistol continued to snarl, baring his teeth behind him. Phillip continued, "Look, I personally think you should have been locked up in jail long ago, but there's no getting around this island would fall apart without you. You run the main source of labor and food for everyone who lives here, and no one can control those men of yours like you can. Maybe it's naïve, but I really hope this lesson might help you change your behavior."

"Because if it doesn't, I'm coming back when he's not around to save your fat ass!" Pistol pulled up on the shore to lean over the edge. His dorsal fin cut the air, and his teeth bared. "And you better believe that I'm going to be around a lot more often."

Phillip lifted an eyebrow at that declaration, but let it be for now. His sudden courage was about to leave at any moment. "What do you say, Boris?"

"I say help me to the damn doctor so he can set my leg," Boris snarled. "Now!"

"Sir?" Phillip questioned. "I'd be happy to help you, but I'd really like your word on this whole thing first."

"Fine! No more trying to capture your little merman," Boris said, rubbing a hand through his thick hair. He was a patient man. He could wait. Boris eyed Chisholm closely, and noticed the tremors at the tips of his fingers. There was plenty of time. "I'll stick with my old fashioned methods."

It was compromise, but for now, Phillip would take it. He reached for Boris, allowing the man to use his shoulder as a crutch. The candlemaker let out a huff of air when the man's full weight leaned on him. *I need to work out,* Phillip thought, and steadied himself before they started to move away from the inlet.

"I better see him later," Pistol warning, pointing straight at Boris. He blinked, retracting the black membrane from his eyes and ducked under the water. He watched through the blue as Phillip helped the oaf balance enough to start dragging themselves to the doctor living just outside the fishery.

Pistol followed unnoticed under along the river, just in case.

CHAPTER 10

THREE DAYS LATER, Boris was in a cast and Phillip was adjusting to being fired.

Boris wanted nothing to do with Phillip or his merman, who true to his word could be seen hanging about the fishery whenever Phillip was there at work. Pistol had taken to eating the fish and generally scaring the workers much to both Phillip and Boris' annoyance. Poor Mark still couldn't go anywhere near the docks without screaming at every little break in the water. So, Boris had Phillip pack up his candles and supplies, and promptly kicked him out the door.

"I'll still buy your candles, Chisholm, but you sure as hell aren't making them here any longer!" Boris had said, slamming the door in his face.

Mark had been kind enough though to help Phillip carry the heavier pots and equipment to his house. How someone could be that considerate and still have the ability to break someone's arm on command still baffled the poor candlemaker. At least he made the work go faster, making good use of his overflowing muscles. Phillip's equipment now sat stacked in a corner, useless in such a tight space. He had thrown a tarp over the lot of it and wondered if he should try and build a small shed or something on the side of his house for a new workshop.

The sound of Icarus giggling brought Phillip out from his worries. He smiled at the boy playing with a ball near the water's edge. Sarah watched from a barrel seat near the dock, fanning herself with a rolled up newsprint. She kept a sharp eye on the boy as he played with Pistol, but it was hardly needed. Icarus would toss the ball to the merman in the water, and he would flick it back with his tail. It was fairly harmless fun, all considered.

Phillip couldn't remember the last time he saw his little boy laugh so much, chasing a small red ball.

"You sure he's safe?" Sarah asked as Phillip came to stand beside her.

"I'm pretty sure he won't hurt Icarus, yes." Phillip rubbed his chest where it had finally started to scar over properly after being reopened so many times. The skin was red and raw around the edges, and Phillip had no doubt he'd have those five marks for the rest of his life. He lifted his hand to cup the shark's tooth and hold it to his chest. "I don't think we have anything to worry about."

"Daddy!" Icarus said, running over with his ball clamped in a tiny, chubby hand. He waved his arm in the air at his father before turning back to the merman laughing in the water. "Look! Look!"

"I see your ball, Icarus. Are you having fun?" Phillip laughed.

"No!" Icarus stomped his foot. He pulled at his father's shirt and dragged him over to the water's edge as it lapped at the sand. Icarus squatted and stuck his stub next to Pistol's. "Look! Same!"

"Oh, wow! How did I not see that?" Phillip knelt lifting his little boy in his arms. There on his little stub, was a brass covering that matched Pistol's fitted neatly over Icarus' bandages. Phillip looked over at the merman, who was very much not looking back at him. He made note to thank him later in private when he wasn't so embarrassed over his own kindness. Phillip rubbed noses with his baby boy. "You're the same! How neat is that?"

"It means he's a tough little thing like me," Pistol said, a touch of pride in his voice. The decorative covering wasn't a kindness, it was a necessity! Bandages were too crude for a strong little kid like that. Pistol licked his lips and pulled at Phillip's socks. "You sure he's your kid?"

"No!" Sarah shouted from the other side, leaning against her barrel. She laughed as Phillip turned red as a beet and whipped around to gape at her. She smirked, reaching down for a bite of cheese she had packed in their picnic. Sarah crossed her legs and cut off a small square to stick in her mouth. "He's not."

"Sarah!"

"Oh! So it is an open marriage? You really should have told him that."

"Stygian?" Phillip stumbled back and fell over, butt falling into the sand when the woman dragged herself up on the beach. Icarus giggled from the fall and settled himself in his father's lap as the woman clung to his arm. Phillip glanced to the shore to see Sarah straighten immediately at the sign of the naked woman draping herself on her husband. The gaping mouth and wide eyes would have been funny, if he wasn't suddenly horrified for his safety.

Phillip may have forgotten to mention Stygian had come back for the final fight.

"You tease, Phillip!" Stygian laughed, poking the little child in the nose. She protected the little one's innocence by making sure her breasts stayed flat against the candlemaker. She rubbed his stomach. "Well, if she can cheat, I don't know why you can't either!"

"We talked about this!" Phillip's voice squeaked, pulling Icarus away from the naked woman. He was too young for this. Phillip was to male for this. And Sarah was climbing off the barrel. For a brief second, Phillip would have given anything to be back in Boris' office with the hot wax. "This is completely inappropriate!"

"I agree," Sarah said. She stalked over to the two and made a show of yanking Phillip back and pulling her son up into her arms in a single swoop. "He's taken."

"Oh? Too bad," Stygian winked, flicking her tentacles on the beach end. She wrapped a strand of blonde hair around her finger, and straightened her back. "Let me know if you change your mind. I'll be around."

"The nerve of some hussies," Sarah grumbled as she stomped back to the house. She dropped Phillip's collar and let him fall back to the beach. "Let's go inside, Icarus. You shouldn't be around women like that." Sarah kicked her husband in the side. "Don't be late!"

Sarah stomped up the beach, Icarus in one arm and her skirt lifted off the ground with the other. If Phillip hadn't known better, he would have thought Sarah was jealous.

"Wow, green-eyed, much?" Pistol whistled. He shoved his friend in the side. "Lucky man."

Phillip splashed Pistol in the face with a handful of water. Icarus laughed over his mother's shoulder.

The sky turned from a warm red to deep, sparkling blue. Icarus had been put to bed with Sarah a few hours ago. Phillip would have joined them, but he could hear the ocean waters moving from his house. Oddly restless from the excitement and too soon calm, he took a stroll back out to the beach. He sat under the edge of the aging dock, letting the waves sooth his nerves after the stressful week. Phillip rolled his shark's tooth in his fingers as he sat, knees tucked up to his chin in the sand. The water danced near his toes, going in and out, wetting the tips of his shoes.

Phillip really did love the water.

It was ever moving, calming, and deceptive with the sheer amount of life it had in it. For example, the merman who had just poked his head up above the surface of the moving waves. Pistol pulled himself up on the beach, lying on his belly next to Phillip. Pistol's tail flipped back and forth, tip still in the water. Phillip's pectoral and back fins were spread eagle on the sand and the grains stuck to the rough surface of his sandpaper skin, coating him in the granules.

It made Phillip itch just looking at him. "Don't you ever go home?"

"Home is boring," Pistol said. He flicked a shell with the edge of his claw. It was calm, and quiet here. No fighting, no Stygian demanding he give up his things, and no Slate looming at his back waiting for Pistol to screw up. No, it was just him, the warm sand, and too good for his own health candlemaker who'd even stand up to his murderous boss. Pistol grinned to himself. *Yeah, this is way more fun.* "I think I'd rather hang out here with you for a while. Gotta' live up to my new name, after all."

"Oh?" Phillip asked. He reached down to pull off his shoes and socks. He pushed his feet forward into the water. They sat alongside Pistol's tail, and he squished his toes in the wet sand. "Where did you hear about a new name?"

"I haven't spent all my time following you. I've been swimming around, you know?" Pistol smacked Phillip's legs with his tail, splashing water up on the man's pants. Phillip laughed and Pistol chuckled alongside him. "But really, the docks are the best, because those losers do nothing but gossip. And let's face it, you are the talk of the town, which means that I'm talk of the town."

"And what does this have to do with your new name?" Phillip asked.

"Well, since old Boris refuses to call me by name and you don't talk to those idiots, they had to come up with something to call me!" Pistol said, smirking. "And I do so hate to disappoint the expectations of my fans."

Phillip snorted at Pistol's tone of voice. He covered his mouth and shook his head. "And what name would that be?"

"The candlemaker's merman."

Phillip fell on his back laughing, with the moon above and his new friend sniggering next to him on the beach. His wife was being nicer, his kid was looking happier every day, and Phillip didn't have to answer to Boris daily any longer. The candlemaker grinned, lying next to his merman.

He could see good things coming on the horizon.

Acknowledgements

To God be the glory forever, and ever, Amen.

As always: Thanks to God in the highest for the talent to write, and the push He gave to everyone who inspired me, helped me, and encouraged me. And of course, thanks be to God for giving us Jesus, who loves you & me.

At this particular moment: I want to thank everyone for reading! Every book purchased and read is one more step toward a lifetime of sharing stories, and I couldn't ask for anything better.

I also want to thank my parents and friends for their continued support, of which I appreciate daily. So thank you!

About The Author

Grey Liliy is a young woman who claims the East Coast of Virginia as her home. She enjoys anime, video games, movies, novels, and comics of just about any genre. Liliy has been drawing & writing a comic of her own since 2005, called *The Adventures of Wiglaf and Mordred*, which you can find at http://liliy.net/wam. Her debut novel, *Children of Hephaestus* was published in September 2012 and is available now.

www.ingramcontent.com/pod-product-compliance
Lightning Source LLC
Chambersburg PA
CBHW052143220626
47052CB00005B/1175